CORRUPTACY

Don VanLandingham

Corruptacy

Don VanLandingham

ISBN (Print Edition): 978-1-09836-154-9

ISBN (eBook Edition): 978-1-09836-155-6

Certificate of Registration Number: TXu 2-232-229 : 1-4-2021

Table of Contents

FOREWORD

A forensic accountant discovers during a bankruptcy fraud investigation, a plot by two high-ranking government officials with ties to a terrorist organization.

More than a mystery, this is a lesson in how bankruptcy does, and doesn't work in the United States. What happens to the money collected? Who are the Trustees? Who are the Judges? How do these people get their jobs? Are there safeguards against abuse? Who is in charge?

"Corruptacy" is a historic novel with a silver lining that can inspire anyone who believes that good will overcome evil.

ABOUT THE AUTHOR

Don VanLandingham is a retired accountant with over forty years of experience as a CPA, specializing in forensic accounting. Before he retired in 2001, he was a member of the American Institute of CPAs, the Association of Certified Fraud Examiners, and an active member of the Georgia Society of CPA's. His engagements to uncover fraud and abuse included national, state, and local governments, in addition to private businesses and nonprofit institutions.

Early in his career, he was appointed as a Chapter 13 Trustee, a position he held for sixteen years. Following the consolidation of his case load into a larger system, he was selected by the Justice Department to examine selected bankruptcy trustees.

Don is married to Linda, his wife of over thirty years. They have six children, five grandchildren, and seven great-grandchildren. They live in the North Georgia Mountains.

AUTHOR'S NOTE

I would like to make something very clear from the outset. This is a novel, not a history lesson. This is neither an indictment of the bankruptcy system that exists today, nor a history lesson regarding the system that existed in the past. This is the story of a young man who began his career as an agnostic, but because of his life experiences of success, failure, love, hate, fear, triumph, and even murder, came to realize a power greater than himself was in control of his destiny.

There is so much I owe to so many people that I'm hesitant to mention them for fear of leaving someone out. So, I will mention only my primary partners.

To my dear friends, Leland and Margie Fay who poured hours into this work, helping me to put meat on the bones of the characters, and kept a non-lawyer straight and on track regarding legal issues. Thank you, both.

I would, however, be remiss not to credit my wife, Linda, for her unfailing love and patience with me as I had her read each chapter time and time again, and for putting up with me for ignoring her, sometimes for hours, during my writing of this novel.

Thank you, sweetheart!
Don VanLandingham

CHAPTER 1

First Real Assignment

I'm on a Delta flight, going from Atlanta, Georgia to Portland Maine. The flight is somewhere over and near Gainesboro, Tennessee where I was born and raised. My name is Jeffrey Cordell Allan and I am an investigative forensic Certified Public Accountant for the EOUST, which, in plain English, are the abbreviations standing for the Executive Office of United States Trustees. The EOUST is actually located in Washington, D.C., but I'm allowed to work out of my home in Helen, Georgia. I live there because I was born in the South, love the mountains, and fishing and tubing where I can relax and get away from my highly stressful job.

Where I grew up in Jackson County, Tennessee, my neighbors and friends didn't use the word forensic, so to them I guess they really didn't understand my job, but in my field of expertise it is used to describe the application of scientific knowledge to legal and accounting problems. What all of this means to me is using my computer and technological knowledge to look for fraud and corruption in bankruptcy cases.

In my brief career I have found there is a lot of public confusion about just what bankruptcy is. The term and theory of bankruptcy actually had its origination in ancient Hebrew society.

The Bankruptcy Act of 1800 was the first law passed in the United States and that Act primarily applied only to merchants. Today the Bankruptcy Abuse Prevention and Consumer Protection Act is the latest attempt by Congress to address all areas of concern.

Bankruptcy judges are appointed by the US Court of Appeals and preside over all bankruptcy cases.

US Trustees were created by the Bankruptcy Reform Act of 1978 to be responsible for the administration of bankruptcy cases. I work for the Executive Office of United States Trustees.

It has been my experience that most consumer bankruptcies are caused by either credit card abuse or by huge medical bills. Of course, you get the undisciplined consumer also who buys more than he or she can afford. Personal bankruptcies usually fall into one of two sections of the bankruptcy code. There is Chapter 7 which is straight bankruptcy, or Chapter 13 which involves either a partial or complete repayment of debt over a period of time. Both sections require a private Standing Trustee, appointed by the District US Trustee, to administer the case.

My job doesn't take me into areas of debtor fraud, caused by the debtor intentionally buying up to the limit of what creditors would allow him to buy, or hiding assets from creditors, and then declaring bankruptcy. My job takes me into the area of funds paid or seized by Standing Trustees from people who have been unfortunate enough to find themselves at the mercy of the bankruptcy courts, due to their inability or unwillingness to pay their debts.

Since graduating from college and passing my CPA examination, I have been working for two years and, up to now have been low man on the totem pole and thus have only handled routine assignments such as reviewing reports and making notes of significant finds of abuse that may have been uncovered. The stress comes from completing my assignments in the time allotted to me. I don't know what idiot figured out how much time a review should take, but it is obvious to me that whoever set the time budgets either had never worked an actual case review or (more likely) didn't do a thorough job and left out a lot of steps that should have been taken to assure every suspected area of possible fraud or abuse was covered.

The plane's engines drone on and it makes me sleepy. I close my eyes and think of my girl friend, Rebecca Stewart, and look forward to my seeing her on my return trip from Portland to Washington where she works as an attorney for an upscale Washington firm. I met Becca four years ago when we were students at Georgetown University, I in the School of Business and she in Pre-law. We've been dating now for a couple of years. We've talked of getting married, but she comes from a broken home and is frightened with the prospects of marriage. I think it will happen one day, but not just yet.

My thoughts now center on my new assignment, and the close call I had in getting here. This is not just a routine assignment. It is my chance to put my investigative skills to work and make a good impression as well as possibly accomplish something that will make a meaningful difference. My boss, EOUST

Director Zack Callahan, spent two hours on the phone with me a week ago outlining his expectations. He had received a detailed confidential letter from Maine Chapter 13 Trustee James Street outlining his suspicions regarding his long-time office manager, Norma Jean Brent.

Callahan decided it was time for me to "earn my wings" so he assigned the case to me. He told me to report to him at the end of every day, and he expected me to do a thorough job. This was my first real case, so, of course, I was excited.

It was the fall of the year and starting to get cold in Maine, so I packed heavy and carried my laptop computer along with my brief case and suitcase to the airport. I was lucky to get a direct flight to Portland and left my apartment in plenty of time to get to the Atlanta-Hartsfield Airport, and took GA 400 South outside of Cleveland, Georgia. It was starting to get late and the drive so far had been monotonous, but as I passed an overpass, suddenly a huge bolder came crashing through the windshield of my Jeep. It only grazed my arm and landed in the passenger seat, but after stopping, I realized I was lucky to be alive. It was if a powerful, invisible force had protected me. I was wearing my new shades, a gift from me to me, so my eyes were protected from breaking glass. Somehow I came to a stop after pulling off the road and tried to get out of the car, but couldn't. My hands were quivering, stuck to the wheel, and I had no strength to open the door. I was still shaking when a highway patrolman appeared and opened my door. He asked if I was hurt, and I told him I thought I was very lucky to be alive. He went over the entire car for his report and it all checked out. He told me they had other complaints about someone dropping large stones or boulders from the overpass into the traffic below. He took me to a service station where I cleaned up from the broken glass. I looked at my watch and I had less than an hour before my plane was scheduled to leave. My car was still drivable, so, I headed for the airport.

I made it to the gate just as it was closing. After begging to get on the flight, the gate official finally opened the gate and on the airplane I went with my suitcase in one hand and laptop and brief case in the other. Of course, I was the last one on the plane. I looked down the rows and rows of passengers trying to locate my seat, and of course, it was on the very back row. I knew every eye was on me, and everyone looked unfriendly and angry about being held up because I was late. I thought, "You know, I bet I could cheer them up by leading everyone in singing the 'Star Spangled Banner.'" Of course I didn't, but I did think about it.

As I stumbled down the aisle hitting every other isle passenger with either my suitcase or my laptop-briefcase hand, I heard a steward say "He's going to kill a passenger". I looked around and a very nice steward took my suitcase and took it up front, and I made it to my seat without any other disturbance. I was worn out!

After a two-and-a-half hour flight, we made it into Portland, where I picked up my rental car and I checked in at the airport motel. I was looking forward to the next day and meeting Mr. Street and Ms. Brent.

The next morning, I checked out of my motel and drove the twenty-six miles to Brunswick, Maine. James Street greeted me warmly and appeared greatly relieved I was there. When I asked to meet his office manager and assistant, Norma Jean Brent,

Street told me that she hadn't been to work in over a week, but had been seen in town by one of the other lawyer's secretaries. She was neither answering his telephone calls nor would she come to the door when he went to her house. He informed me that the Trustee office was in shambles and in total disarray. He wasn't kidding! All of the computer accounting records, all of the bank statements with the cancelled checks and deposit slips were gone. So was the most current Receipts Book. Fortunately, Street had all of the previous Receipt Books locked in his office safe, so all we would permanently lose in records were the past three weeks. There were potentially thousands of documents that had to be reconstructed into a meaningful record. It looked like a challenging task was in front of me.

I was not convinced Street is the paragon of virtue he makes himself out to be. Why did he wait so long to notify the Director of the missing records? I mean, in my suspicious mind, he and Ms. Brent could have cooked this whole thing up. Street and I went to the bank where the account was handled, talked to the local president of the bank, and explained the dilemma. What would it take for the bank to look up the microfilm records of all the transactions and print them out for me to re-construct a record of each debtor's account? The bank was willing to spend their resources, but it would take a good month to produce all of the transactions.

Street looked genuinely relieved (which made me feel somewhat more confident in his integrity). Norma Jean Brent was first on my list of people I wanted to interview, but she remained unavailable. I was somewhat intrigued with her first name, it being the original name of a famous Hollywood starlet.

Street hired a young lady the bank President recommended, beginning the process of handling the Trusteeship's day-to-day transactions. I made my plane reservations to fly to Washington to meet with the Director, said goodbye to Street for now, and headed back to Portland and the airport.

CHAPTER 2

Her Candle Burned Out

Three months later, I'm back in Brunswick. It is the middle of winter. Temperature in the low forties, but further inland, there's snow on the ground. The trees, which had been at their autumn best when I was here before, are now naked of leaves. After I had previously left here (it seems like a year ago), I had a three day meeting with Director Callahan in Washington where we planned in detail my Brunswick engagement. Of course, I spent every free minute with Becca where we enjoyed each other's company immensely. One night we drove to Annapolis Maryland and had a great dinner of crabs at O'Leary's Seafood Restaurant. We sat next to a couple from the Naval Academy and we enjoyed immensely our conversations with them. I got tickled at Becca's attempts to split open the crabs with a hammer. The shell exploded and went everywhere, including on the shirts of the cadets we had just met. Fortunately, they were good sports about it all. Another evening we went to Glenn Echo Amusement Park where we acted like teenagers riding every ride we could. Life with Rebecca could be so good if only we didn't have to part at nighttime.

Knowing that the Brunswick, Maine bank would take a while to complete their copying job, I was sent to the office of another bankruptcy trustee in Newark, New Jersey to do a preliminary study whether to begin another investigation by either myself or another EOUST employee of that office. I was able to determine that there was a reasonable chance that a thorough investigation might reveal another case of fraud or abuse by a Trustee.

Returning to my home in Helen was always the best part of every trip. I took a week off. I spent every day either by fishing in one of several creeks that eventually made their way to the Chattahoochee River or by tubing down that same river which flowed through the middle of the town.

Helen Georgia was originally a lumber town. Like so many small towns in those days in the sixties, Helen had been dying a slow and painful death. Then, a group of businessmen got together and devised a plan that would eventually turn Helen into a Swiss-like Bavarian alpine village and become Georgia's third most visited city with great restaurants, outdoor recreation activities and friendly shop-owners. All of these benefits of a small community were why I chose it a couple of years ago to be my home.

But fun time was now over and I realize I am in Brunswick as I begin to concentrate on my formidable task of preparing to present evidence to a Federal Grand Jury. A week after I left here previously, someone tried to burn the office down. The Trustee's office is located on the second floor of a former family residence on a main street in Brunswick. A set of wooden stairs located at the rear of the building on the outside leading up to the second floor is where people who had bankruptcy business were expected to access the office without having to go through the front door. People were encouraged to use these stairs so they wouldn't disturb the clients of the other attorneys in the firm in the waiting room at the front entrance. It was at these back stairs that someone started the fire in the middle of the night. Luckily, a neighbor spotted the smoke and called the fire department before the fire reached the top floor, but the stairs were damaged beyond repair. Suspicion was directed toward the still absent Ms. Brent, but as of yet, there was no evidence directly implicating her. She had been visited by FBI agents who almost had to break down the door before she would finally answer it, and then they questioned her about both the missing Trustee records and the suspicious fire. She denied having anything to do with the any of that and threatened suit against them if they reported that she was a suspect.

There was a lot of office gossip about Norma Jean Brent particularly from the other secretaries in the law office of Southerland, Harris and Street. I interviewed each of the secretaries, and according to them, Norma Jean Brent had always dressed extremely elegantly, even when coming to work. She wore expensive jewelry, which raised curiosities given her humble background. She was married to a career naval officer who was assigned to the Brunswick Naval Air Station. He was paid well but not to the level of affluence his wife was living. During the times he was away on assignments, she had been seen in a nearby town in the company of other naval officers in one of the many saloons the town had to offer. The Big Question was and always had been: Where did she get the money to enjoy the life style she was living? Tongues were wagging as she sashayed on.

The bank's employees had done their part very well. I had been given copies of every check, bank statement, and deposit slip for the past three years, which was what I had asked for. In my reconstruction of individual trustee records, I was able to determine that there were receipts totaling in excess of $37,000 that did not get deposited to the Trustee's bank account. I had the details of the missing funds included in my report and submitted it to Washington headquarters while I was still in Brunswick. The report was approved by the EOUST, and they had forwarded a copy to the Department of Justice, which would be prosecuting the case against Norma Jean Brent. I was still in Brunswick at the request of the Director, to assist the Trustee and help re-establish trust with the bankruptcy community (court and attorneys). I expected and received a grand-jury summons to testify on behalf of the United States.

That night, Trustee Street and his wife Brenda took me to Taste of Maine Seafood Restaurant located just on the other side of the Kennebec River just north of Bath Maine for a much-awaited treat at destroying some lobsters. Lobsters are never cheap, even in Maine, but they are fresh, and restaurants there know how to prepare them. The restaurant was rather crowded, but the wait was well worth it. James Street knew many of the patrons in the restaurant and several came over to the table and chatted. Most of our table visitors knew about Norma Jean Brent and what had taken place which was not surprising because I had been able to discern that Brunswick is a close-knit community and secrets are scarce. Without giving them any details, James told them I was the one responsible for restoring order to his office. I blushed with pride.

The restaurant's special tonight was three lobsters for the price of two, so, we all splurged and got the special. Afterwards we talked and laughed at some of the more colorful aspects of the case that seemed so unsolvable just three months ago. In those three months, I had become more confident in James Street's integrity and honesty, even though I still had reservations about his inexperience and casualness in perceiving and evaluating suspicious occurrences. I wrote in my report that he needed to be made more aware of the necessity of reviewing the work of his employees.

That night I lay awake in my bed at the motel I was staying at. I was nervous about my appearance in court the next morning. This would be my first time in a courtroom since that disastrous appearance I made five years ago in a courtroom in Washington, D.C. Now before I begin to tell you what happened in that instance, you need to know something about my early life.

My parents were good people, but they had difficult problems. Dad had contacted polio as a child, and he spent most of his life in a wheel chair. He held the office of County Clerk of Court for twenty years, but had to retire when he became so incapacitated because of the polio, he could not do his work. He died shortly afterwards of cardiac arrest when I was sixteen years old. Mom had to go to work and I was left to soak up knowledge, experience, and wisdom wherever I could find it. I was a poor student and spent most of my time in class daydreaming about what I was going to do after school. I enjoyed playing pranks, like the time I and a buddy placed a purse loaded with cow dung out on the highway. We laughed like crazy when a car picked it up-- went about 100 yards down the road, stopped, and, driver cursing like a sailor, threw it back out on the road for someone else to stop and go through the same smelly trial that he had. Looking back on that now I was surprised someone hadn't shot us!!

One of my teachers told my mom that I was a dreamer, while another wrongly accused me of plagiarizing a novel I had been assigned to write. I rewrote the novel and made it bad on purpose so she would get off my back. I remember the result was I received a D- grade in that course. Socially and sports wise, I didn't date much and considered myself a poor athlete, although I did excel in track, placing third in the Tennessee High School State finals in the mile, which I finished in 4:32. I truly loved baseball but was not gifted in that sport. I developed a "win at any cost" mentality which suited me fine as long as I could get away with it. Fortunately, the FBI background investigation didn't turn up anything too derogatory, like the prank I pulled with the cow dung; otherwise, I probably wouldn't have gotten my job with them. After two years of clerking, I was ready for something different, a bigger challenge. I was a student at Georgetown and through their placement office I got a job with Benedict Frozen Foods, a rather shady freezer-food company. I discovered they hired fast talking salesmen who would say anything to get the customer to invest their food money in a three-month supply of frozen food. Unfortunately, most of the buyers were poor families who were easily convinced to sign on the dotted line for a freezer full of food. Unfortunately, most ate all of the steaks in the first month, and so they had no cuts of good beef to last them the final two months until their next order. As a result, many stopped making their monthly or weekly payments, and then our collection agency man would file liens against them. Some of these actions would take the consumers into civil court where the company presented an air-tight case. All the consumers could say was they had run out of meat, and they weren't supposed to, they thought.

One day, on a rather circumstantial case, the collection manager asked me to go to court to testify. I told him I really didn't know much about the case, but he insisted that I could really help his case, so to court I went. It almost finished me. I was called to the stand to testify about what little I knew and was asked by the defense attorney if I had witnessed the signature of his client on the bill of sale. Under my "WIN AT ANY COST" attitude, my thinking was, "I have to win this for my company. I have to be the hero." So I answered "Yes." The attorney looked me right in the eye and asked "Are you sure?" Well, I felt I was in too deep now so again I answered "Yes." Everyone in the courtroom knew I was lying because everyone who knew anything about the business knew that the customer's signature didn't need a witness, and that there was no reason for me to be present when the loan agreement was signed. It didn't take long for the judge to render his ruling in favor of the defendant. It was more than just my lying answer that sunk the case. My company's collection guy had gotten confused about some of the other aspects of the case, but my lying testimony didn't help either. That evening I had a class in Commercial Law. I'll never forget how class began that night. Law Professor Randolph Sweeny began his lecture thusly.

"We have among us tonight one of our students who testified in court today and committed perjury by lying on the stand. Everyone knew he was lying. He was even given a chance to recant his lie, but instead lied again. I cannot emphasize this enough. YOU DO NOT EVER DO THAT IF YOU WANT TO AMOUNT TO MORE THAN A HILL OF BEANS!"

That was all he said about the matter. I slumped down in my seat and just knew everyone in the class knew who the jackass liar was. Fortunately, no one fingered me, but I knew and vowed it would never happen to me again. This was a lesson on morality for one who had no early role model.

Now I found myself in a courtroom again and have vowed again to tell the truth, and I did. I described in detail what I knew about the case and the results of my examination. Norma Jean Brent was there with a man who may have been her husband, although he was not in uniform. Later that afternoon, the grand jury returned a "True Bill" which means a majority of the grand jury members felt we had presented enough evidence to refer the case to the US Attorney for prosecution.

The following day would prove to be my next to last in Brunswick. At noon time, the local radio station described a bank robbery in a neighboring town. Police were in pursuit of the robber. I didn't pay much attention to it, but the next morning before I left for the Portland airport to go home, the morning news broadcast gave a strange account of how Norma Jean Brent was the bank robber villain. They went on to give a bizarre description of what had happened. Apparently, Ms. Brent had gone to a local criminal attorney for help in her situation. The attorney told her he would take the case but had to have a retainer of $3,500 before he would lift a finger to help her. Ms. Brent then went to a bank in a neighboring town and handed the teller a note informing the teller that the customer had a gun pointed at her and demanded $3,500 in small bills. Of course, the teller obliged and as Ms. Brent left the building, the teller rang the alarm. Ms. Brent sped away in her red Oldsmobile convertible driving at eighty to ninety miles an hour down the freeway with police chasing her. Thinking that all they wanted was the money, she threw it out of the window; but, of course, the chase ended as you might predict. Now Norma Jean Brent faced new and potentially more damaging charges, and it would end up costing her a lot more than $3,500!

After I got home, a few weeks later, I received a phone call from James Street informing me that Norma Jean Brent had been found guilty of embezzling funds from his office, but not guilty of bank robbery by reasons of insanity.

Goodbye, Norma Jean.

CHAPTER 3

Politics, Prejudices, and Conflicting Personalities

Bankruptcy in the United States is a big deal. A very BIG DEAL. Willie Sutton, the notorious bank robber from the last century was once asked, "Why do you rob banks?" His answer famously, "Because that's where the money is!"

The bankruptcy system is the very embodiment of Mr. Sutton's well-known dictum. Currently pending are hundreds of thousands of cases with money described as "in the billions." Connected with those billions is a pile of fees that flows to the people associated with it; consultants, accountants, and of course, lawyers. Then there are those who work for them and advise them. Clearly, the bankruptcy system is at the core of America's economic system.

The administration of bankruptcy laws is, for forty-eight of the fifty states, a responsibility of the Department of Justice. Prior to 1978, all bankruptcy matters were handled by the judicial arm of government. Bankruptcy judges had been solely responsible for administration of their cases and for the selection of Trustees.

Then in 1978, Congress passed the "Bankruptcy Reform Act." This important change established the administrative arm of the entire system, the US Trustee System. Only two Southern States (North Carolina and Alabama) opted out of the system. This was the first introduction of politics into bankruptcy administration, but would not be the last.

Chapter 13 is different from other forms of bankruptcy because it deals with a personal bankruptcy procedure where a debtor can get relief of his debts by agreeing to pay to the Trustee an agreed upon amount, set by the bankruptcy court, and then the Trustee disburses that money to the debtor's creditors in amounts set by the court. What most people don't know is anything about the Trustee, either his character or his track record. Chapter 13 Trustees are supposed to be selected based on the educational and/or prior work experience. Usually, there is only one Chapter 13 Trustee for a geographical area, like a large city or a set section of a state. Many times, a Chapter 13 case load is large enough that a Chapter 13 Trustee devotes his entire working life to his Chapter 13 case load. When debtors pay their hard-earned money to a bank, they usually have the reputation earned by the banking institution to guide them in their trust. However, when they pay their money to a court appointed individual "Trustee," they only have their faith in the system to comfort them. That is why it is so important to the integrity of the system to oversee the Trustees and make sure safeguards are in place. That was one of the main purposes of the 1978 Bankruptcy Act. Chapter 13 Trustees are not employees of the government. They are private individuals mostly engaged in the practice of law, accounting, or a similar field. They are selected by the US Trustees to administer cases in that US Trustee Region.

All Trustees must undergo an FBI background examination. Once appointed, they serve at the pleasure of the US Trustee in that Region. The volume of cases that travel through a Trustee's office depends on the region. For instance, just about every Chapter 13 Trustee in Tennessee has thousands of cases. Not so in New York where past due debts are more difficult to resolve because of liberal laws protecting delinquent debtors at the expense of their creditors. Consequently, it would be unusual for a Trustee in New York to have more than a few hundred cases.

The Trustees are compensated by a percentage of their collections. This percentage is set by the US Trustee. The Trustees must undergo an annual audit examination by CPA firms selected by the US Trustee. In addition he must endure annual inspection tours.

The US Trustees, on the other hand, are attorneys selected by the Attorney General. Most of the times, the selections were made without political pressure. However, there are times the Attorney General was leaned on by members of Congress anxious to satisfy some political favor. US Trustees have been appointed by Senators asking for and getting a favor for a family member or a friend of some generous contributor.

Up until now, my career with EOUST had been generally free from politics, prejudices, and conflicting personalities within the department.

This was about to change.

After a couple of weeks off following the Maine case, I was assigned to the Region 8 District covering Tennessee and Kentucky. I was ordered to report to the US Trustee, who was an ex-college football star named Rocky Spradlin. Reliable gossip reported his appointment had been made under the influence of a current United States Senator.

Spradlin, at 6 foot 7 inches towered above everyone and relied on his stature and loud, booming voice of intimidation to get what he wanted.

He was a bully.

My assignment was to conduct inspection tours of the Chapter 13 Trustees in Region 8, along with US Trustee Spradlin. This was a rather typical assignment for one in my position, so it was run-of-the-mill duty.

I landed Monday morning at the Memphis International Airport and was picked up by a clerk from the UST office and taken to a professional looking high-rise building on Madison Avenue.

After being lectured about expected outcomes by Trustee Spradlin, we began our tour at the Memphis office of the Chapter 13 Trustees. Because of the large number of cases here, there are actually two Trustees for Memphis. They share office space, computer systems, and sometimes employees.

At noontime, Spradlin announced he was taking us to lunch. This included his two administrative assistants, me and him. Of course, he meant Barbeque because we were in Memphis. He told me we were going to the Rendezvous, well-known for their "Dry Ribs." We piled in there at lunch and were told it was closed on Monday's. Rocky explained in his usual loud, over-bearing voice, that we had come from hundreds of miles away to enjoy their ribs, and we weren't going away until we were seated. The manager showed up and finally agreed to seat us. I learned later that Rocky's flair up at the restaurant greeter was just for show as he had made an earlier call to the owner to arrange for us to eat there, even though they were closed. Rocky ordered for everyone, which included me and the two ladies from the office. I had the pork ribs, dry rub style, and they were fantastic. They were well seasoned and peppered with lots of Rocky's "war stories." I realized this was a performance by the host Trustee and we were all supposed to be impressed.

Towards the end of the meal, Rocky went to the restroom just as the check arrived. Before leaving to resume our tour, Rocky ordered a whole pecan pie to go and asked the waiter to put the pie on the check, which I was in the process of paying. I ended up putting the whole lunch on my personal credit card, something I would have to explain to Zack Callahan later.

That afternoon we left for Jackson, Tennessee, a couple of hours to the East of Memphis. Tennessee is a long, skinny state with I-40 running the entire length, more than 400 miles with five major cities hanging off it like trout on a stringer. From Jackson we went to Nashville, Chattanooga, Knoxville, and finally on Friday to Kingsport. We were able to conquer Tennessee in five days because I had told each Trustee what our expectations were and what preparations were required of them. It was pretty standard stuff for an accountant.

Since we drove together in Rocky's Jaguar, he was my constant companion during the day. That meant three meals a day.

Every time I tried to convince myself that he wasn't really such a bad guy, he would insult me or someone else. I kept mostly to myself during his monologues, except when he started to tell an off-color story or "joke." Then I cut him off quickly.

We did about one office per day, and it was exhausting, particularly having to change motel rooms every day and having to listen to Rocky's constant war stories.

It was at Kingsport, Tennessee that I really got my next reality check.

Before beginning my inspection, Trustee Spradlin pulled me aside and told me that the Kingsport Trustee was an incompetent nincompoop, engendering numerous complaints, and justifying replacement. He tried to intimidate me by insisting that my written report of the inspection must reflect that reality. I looked Spradlin right in the eye and told him that we would let the facts speak for themselves.

One of the things that Spradlin didn't like was that the Kingsport Trustee used a different software system from the other Tennessee Trustees. His system didn't have all of the "bells and whistles" the other systems had, but it appeared from every test I ran that it was sufficient. I audited a sample of his cases and found that this Trustee was actually more efficient than some of the other larger Trustees. This was probably because of the smaller case load this Trustee had in comparison with the other Tennessee Trustees. This Trustee handled the Appalachian Mountain territory from just east of Knoxville then north to the Virginia line. Spradlin asked me to let him see my report before I sent it in to make sure it was accurate. I told him his request was against my instructions I had been given by Callahan, and he became indignant

This set off a signal to me that something was wrong with him. I was really grateful about a lesson my daddy taught me years before, to trust my "internal warning system." That would prove invaluable later. My daddy used to call this type of warning my "bunk-o-meter" and that I should pay attention to it. It didn't mean that I shouldn't trust people, but because many people have a propensity to bend the truth, it was our responsibility to be able to discern the truth.

By late Friday afternoon, we had completed our assigned work and my UST companion couldn't wait to be rid of me. I was going to Cookeville to spend the weekend with my sister Peggy and her family. Spradlin was going to Monterey which was several miles from Cookeville. Rather than drive me to Cookeville, Spradlin said he wasn't going any further than Monterey and that Peggy could come and pick me up. Things like that can tell you a lot about someone's character.

I owe so much to my sister. She is eight years older than I am and she basically raised me. She had to temporarily quit school and went to work at a yarn mill to help support me and my mother after Dad died. She later got a scholarship to go to college there in Cookeville at Tennessee Tech. After graduation she got her teacher's certificate and has taught High School Math and Sunday School ever since. Her husband, Bill, is an engineer and works in near Knoxville in Oak Ridge in a nuclear reactor laboratory. I reminded myself what a wonderful and kind woman she is and it was great to be with her and her family. We spent a most enjoyable weekend touring lakes and waterfalls I hadn't seen in years.

Saturday and Sunday were a great break for me away from the self-centered Rocky Spradlin. Sunday evening, I drove the three hours it took to Lexington, Kentucky where the first of two Kentucky Trusteeships were located.

Early Monday morning I received some unofficial instructions from Spradlin. He looked hung over and didn't want to talk much which was refreshing. He did say he wanted me to "dig up dirt" on the Lexington guy because, in Spradlin's words, he wasn't a "team player."

This Trusteeship didn't use a computer system at all. His staff kept all records by hand. It appeared to work because, just like the Kingsport guy, the case load was in the hundreds and not the thousands. The samples I chose were as clean as falling snow. The Trustee and his staff were very efficient and organized, and I wrote my report accordingly. From there we went to Louisville where the case load was much greater, and they used the same computer system as the larger Trustees in Tennessee used. The Chapter 13 Trustee was a very attractive lady whom Rocky immediately took a liking to. He spent most of his time with her in her office, and later told me what a wonderful Trustee she was. I pulled my sample of cases and found several irregularities. Nothing to suggest misappropriation of funds, but rather a general sloppiness which we could correct with some simple procedural improvements. I prepared my report noting the problems. I had no further contact with Spradlin, and when I completed my report, I drove to the airport for my trip back home. My plan was to complete my reports there and send my reports on to Washington.

About a week later, I got a phone call from Zack Callahan instructing me to come to Washington for a conference with the Director and UST Spradlin. Sitting in the conference room was the stone-faced Spradlin who wouldn't look directly at me. After Director Callahan came in and I was forced to endure Spradlin's lies and half-truths for about an hour, I finally got to tell my side. I did not argue. I read from my notes and the reports I had sent in. Spradlin denied everything he had told me which I had expected him to do. It was clearly up to Callahan to evaluate the two stories. Spradlin glared at me then left the room leaving me and Director Callahan alone. Finally, Callahan told me that he admired me for taking the stand I had taken, and that he had been led to believe by the Attorney General that Spradlin's days were numbered.

Next, I was sent to Salt Lake City, Utah to review some of the cases of a Chapter 13 Trustee who was under investigation for "gross incompetence." That was a code term used to describe a Trustee they thought was dishonest, but they didn't have enough evidence against him or her to convict. According to Callahan, The US Trustee wasn't reassigning her active cases; she just wasn't being assigned any new cases. The new cases were all going to a just named newly appointed Chapter 13 Trustee. My big question was why weren't all of her remaining cases assigned to the newly appointed Trustee? I never received a satisfactory answer.

I conducted the inspection without a US Trustee breathing down my neck all the time telling me what to find. It took two days. The problems I found didn't begin to approach some of my findings in Tennessee or Kentucky. I completed my written report from home and mailed it to Callahan. If I was hoping for a good reaction from the US Trustee, again I would be disappointed. I had another US Trustee screaming for my scalp.

I found out a couple of weeks later from some UST employees that US Trustee Spradlin had promised the two Trusteeships in Tennessee and Kentucky to a couple of college frat brothers of his. The Quid Pro Quo was that the frat brother who was trying to get his two friends a lucrative government job was a US Senator who had arraigned to have Spradlin appointed several years before. Spradlin was canned, and those appointments never took place. It took me a while longer, but I found out that the Utah US Trustee replaced a non-Mormon with a member from his Mormon church. He got away with it.

Afterwards, I got sent out on a really strange case.

A CPA in auditing a Chapter 13 Trustee in Jackson Mississippi was having a difficult time completing his assignment of auditing the records. The audit fieldwork was supposed to have been completed, but the CPA couldn't get his reconciliation of cash receipts to agree with the deposits made to the bank. He had to return to Mississippi and complete his work. That's where the conflict came in. The Trustee, thinking the audit was over had taken all of his records back to his warehouse for storage and didn't want to get them again. The US Trustee couldn't resolve the difference either so he called the Director. My instructions were to resolve their differences and report back to Director Callahan. On the road I went again. This time to Mississippi.

I convinced the Trustee that he had to get the records the auditor needed, and let the accountant finish his work. I was about to leave, but the CPA was clearly confused and mystified by the unresolved difference. So, I took a look at the adding machine tapes made from each day's collections. There was a total printed on the bottom of each tape. I took one and mentally added what was on the tape. My mental math didn't jibe with the total so I took an adding machine and added the numbers on the tape. Lo and behold! The total on my tape was several hundred dollars more than the total shown on the office tape. I pointed that out to the young accountant and together we re-added all of the tapes for a month. Every tape was under-stated! This was a very important find. The printed tape numbers represented the receipt book items, and the total at the bottom of the tape represented what was being deposited to the bank. What was missing was the shortage in the deposit which was covered up by the office employee's manipulation of the adding machine tape.

We talked to the Trustee and then to the woman office employee who prepared the tapes. She finally admitted to doctoring the tapes by scrolling down the tape and imputing a false negative amount representing the missing cash, then by scrolling up again and totaling the tape out. The lesson here is obvious. Never accept as gospel the total on an adding machine tape! I left my relieved CPA friend to complete his report, and reported my findings to the Director and left for home. The Director reported my findings to the US Trustee who was furious that I had not told him what I had found. I did what I was asked to do.

Politics, prejudices, and conflicting personalities. I was pretty well shaken by these experiences, but this was like a brief shower compared with the coming hurricanes I would have to endure.

CHAPTER 4

Whistle Blower

During a gap in the Maine case, I had been sent to Newark, New Jersey to interview a woman who, in a private telephone conversation with Callahan, accused the Trustee in Newark of stealing cash out of her daily receipts. In government parlance, this kind of witness is called a "Whistle Blower." Congress had passed special legislation to protect these people and their testimony to expose corruption and prosecute the wrongdoers.

For the sake of convenience and security, we had met at "Dunkin Donuts" in the Newark airport. It was important for me to spend the time to get to know and understand this woman in order to evaluate her as a potential witness. If the government decided to prosecute the wrongdoer it was important to know what motivated her to take a risk like this. In our conversation, I found out a lot about her, that she was a mother of three small children while her husband was on active duty in Afghanistan. Her mom was taking care of the children and she was finishing her degree in accounting at Montclair State, a tough and expensive school. She was entitled to anonymity until final resolution. I was impressed with what I had learned about her because of the risk she took in coming forward, and I made a decision that she deserved, and would be afforded, protection as much as possible.

Next, she and I discussed her accounting analysis. Because she was studying accounting, she knew I needed to ask about money coming in and going out of the trusteeship. She had brought along some copies of transactions involving office receipts and copies of the corresponding bank deposit slips and they balanced. So what was wrong? She showed me that the receipts reflected hundreds of dollars in cash coming in, but there was very little cash being deposited to the bank as reflected in the copies of bank deposits. She told me that she mentioned her concern to her boss about the unaccounted for cash, but he told her to just ignore it as long as everything balanced. I thanked the lady and returned to Washington to continue to work on the Maine case.

Soon after my experience in Tennessee and Kentucky, I was sent back to New Jersey to continue my examination of the Newark Chapter 13 Trustee. I reviewed my notes of my meeting with the lady "Whistle Blower," and I was determined to find out about the unaccounted for cash. My plane landed in Newark around midnight, and I was really beat and I headed for my hotel room.

The office manager in the Newark UST office had made my travel arrangements. I think he really blew it. My hotel was located in a rather dingy part of town. It was sort of typical for that part of the world where there are too many people living in limited space. The parking lot was located underground and the lighting was almost nonexistent. I parked as close as I could get to the hotel door. Relieved to be in a safe place I went through my nightly ritual of a shower and teeth brushing and laying my stuff out for morning. I was just drifting off when suddenly there was a loud banging on my door. I took a look through the peephole and saw a very attractive red-headed woman. I opened the door a crack and asked what she wanted. She told me she was "Personal Room Service" at my request! Well, I didn't request and she said she had been sent by a "special friend." Again, I declined and she went away, or so I thought. A moment later another knock came from the same woman. "You sure you didn't order this honey because I have something special for you." Trying to be polite I replied "No, thank you, ma'am," and closed the door making sure the bolt was in place. She hollered at me that I didn't know what I was missing as she stormed off down the hall. I didn't sleep much that night fretting over the events of my night in Newark.

The next morning, I checked out. I wasn't going to spend another night like I had just experienced in that hotel. Later that morning I had a chance to tell someone in the office about my experience the night before. He nearly doubled over in laughter and told me that the office's audit staff person pulled that bit of malarkey every time someone new came to the office. I told him I thought Callahan might want to know how Newark personnel were spending their working hours playing games, and I would tell him if I heard of it happening again!

Later that afternoon, I arrived at the Chapter 13 Trustee's office to continue my earlier examination. Trustee Clarence Cobb proudly led me through a comparison of his daily receipt log with the bank deposit amounts shown on the bank statement. On the surface, they appeared to be in order, but when I asked to see copies of his bank deposit slips, he got real testy and finally admitted that he didn't keep copies. My "bunk-o-meter" told me he was lying, so I patiently explained to him that his failure to keep copies of deposit slips was in violation of the Trustee handbook (which he was supposed to have read and complied with). Cobb professed ignorance of the required documentation, but promised he would immediately put the requirements into practice.

Enlisting the help of the US Trustee in Newark he and I went to the bank where the Chapter 13 Trustee had the trust account, and we convinced the branch manager to comply with our request for documents. I was able to obtain a month's worth of copies of deposit slips and the checks making up the deposit slips and immediately went to work. I determined that the copies of checks making up the deposit slips contained some checks which had no relationship to the names of the debtors who were making their payments to the Trustee's office. Most of these maverick checks were from car dealerships and the checks were payable to "Matterhorn Motor Works." On the back of each check was written "Pay to the Order of the Office of the Chapter 13 Trustee," and then a rubber stamp imprint below that of "Matterhorn Motor Works." It was also noted that each deposit slip contained only a small amount of cash, whereas the office receipts records of each day reflected sometimes thousands of dollars of cash. Our "Whistle Blower's" instincts were solid. There was clearly a huge problem.

By this time in my career, I had been given pretty much a free reign to use whatever resources I needed. That evening I called Director Callahan at his home to report my initial findings of missing or unaccounted for cash together with my recommendations. It sounded like Matterhorn Motor Works could be a front for a stolen car ring. This was a criminal matter and beyond either of our expertise. Callahan said this was something for the FBI. With his permission I decided to turn to a local FBI agent, an old friend and former Georgetown classmate, "Fast Eddie" Cruise.

"Fast Eddie" was a nickname Cruise had obtained at Georgetown, not because he was fast with a handgun or even his mouth, but because of his reputation with the ladies. In fact, I've always felt indebted to Eddie because through him I was able to meet and become romantically involved with Rebecca.

During my second year at Georgetown, I went on a date with one of my classmates, and we were eating at Nick's Riverside Grill in old Georgetown when in walked my classmate Eddie Cruise with his date who just happened to be Rebecca. We invited them to sit with us, and it soon became obvious that Rebecca and Eddie were just casual friends as were my date and I. It soon became equally obvious that both Eddie and I were greatly attracted to the other's date, so it didn't take much until we left together, I with Rebecca and "Fast Eddie" with my original date.

Eddie graduated from Georgetown with Honors in Accounting, got his CPA certificate, applied for and was accepted as an FBI agent, and, after spending a couple of years in Kansas City, was transferred to Newark, NJ. We have stayed close by writing and visiting each other through the years. I even was able to convince Eddie (but not his wife) to rent a kayak and cruise down the Chattahoochee River with me once when they visited in Helen. A very settled man, but still cannot shake the nickname that has always followed him, "Fast Eddie."

Funny thing about nick names. Seems they don't always tell the whole story. As Eddie and I got to know each other better, I found out that he obtained the nickname not because of his success with the ladies, but because of his uncanny ability to escape from the ladies. He was handsome and dressed better than most of the other guys. He dated a lot, but never more than a couple of dates with any one girl. Then he was gone, and on to the next girl. Never wanted to get tied down and was very serious about school and the future. That was then. Today, Eddie is very much in love with his wife and his two small children. He is kind and compassionate and a very good friend.

After outlining my findings involving Matterhorn Motor Works to Director Callahan, Eddie and I met at the FBI Field Office in Newark where I laid out my documents, notes, and evidence, being careful of respecting the identity of our "Whistle Blower." Eddie revealed to me that his office had received complaints from local law enforcement officials about a suspected stolen car ring headquartered in Newark, and the FBI had just recently opened a file on the suspected dealer, Matterhorn Motor Works.

Eddie led the FBI investigation, and it was shortly learned that Matterhorn Motor Works was found to be buying hot cars from thieves, giving them forged "clean" registrations. They sold them to legitimate dealers who were making their checks payable to Matterhorn Motor Works. The owner of Matterhorn was giving those checks to Trustee Cobb (who was a primary agent of the conspiracy) who would take cash the debtors had brought to his office and substitute the checks. It had worked for about five years and it looked like they had pocketed about two million dollars, tax free. We both felt this would have been discovered by the US Trustee's staff except one of their own was covering it up.

I found out later that FBI agents raided the offices of the stolen car ring-leader and had found all of the evidence they needed to put these guys away for several years. They found that the scam had been successful because the United States Trustee's audit employee was involved in the crime by being paid to overlook the crime. He was not only fired but also received a ten year sentence. He admitted that he had tried to place me in a compromising position with that red head in the hotel. So, several crimes got solved here; the embezzlement of bankruptcy cash funds; second, a stolen car ring, third; of course, none of the cash received by the bad guys was reported as income, so the IRS got involved and successfully prosecuted five people for tax fraud. A substantial "finders" fee was paid by the IRS to our "Whistle Blower" who was using the fee to complete her education and ultimately get her CPA license. She now works at our Newark UST office, and her husband returned in one piece from his military duty. I was feeling pretty satisfied with the results.

I returned to our Washington, D.C. Headquarters and completed my report, and received the congratulations from the Director and my colleagues. By this time, I was getting quite a reputation as a Crime Buster, and I suppose it went to my head a little. The next case though brought me back to reality and made me realize that I was a player in a dangerous game, one that others were playing for more than just money.

CHAPTER 5

Texas Tragedy

Ever since I began my professional career, I had a very strong, uncanny certainty that one day, I would be at the center of a potentially catastrophic event. I have been continually haunted by this mysterious feeling. I had no idea what that event would be or where the source was, but I have asked myself repeatedly, "Is this the job I am destined to do that would lead me to that catastrophic event?" I strongly believed I had been destined for some great moment that would be really meaningful, but I was not sure I was on the right path for that meaningful moment we all dream about.

"You're going to Amarillo, Texas, Allan." The second time Callahan said it I let the words sink in. He only called me by my last name when he wanted to give me an unarguable directive. I gave him my complete attention.

"We have a potential problem with the Chapter 7 Trustee in Amarillo that might involve illegal drugs coming in from Mexico."

I asked him why was I the one being sent to Amarillo.

"You're pretty good about sniffing out fraud, kind of like I was at your age."

High praise, indeed, coming from that man!

"I think you've got a nose for this stuff. Your assignment, though, is limited to an examination of financial transactions. Nothing else. There will be a DEA man assigned to work with you. If he wants to involve you in anything regarding his particular assignment, you are to tell him he would have to contact me first."

Well, this assignment was not what I signed up for, but my respect for Zack Callahan had grown from being just a boss in the beginning to now being a mentor. He seems to have taken a liking to me like no other older man had done since my Dad died years before. I never really got to know my Dad, and then he died before we had a chance to become really good friends.

Callahan had become like the father I had wished I still had. He counseled and challenged me, not only professionally, but also in my personal life. He taught me many things that I had to know in order to be a successful accountant as well as a man in this ever-changing world. He was my ideal of what a mentor should be.

Now I jumped into the preparations for my upcoming trip to Amarillo, Texas, and had to dismiss the fears I had about lurking rattle snakes and jumping tarantulas.

A meeting with officials of DEA and UST offices revealed suspicions of a drug cartel possibly laundering their receipts through the Bankruptcy Trustee in Amarillo, kind of like my previous case in Newark. However, if these suspicions proved to be correct, this case would be a lot more dangerous assignment than chasing car crooks in Newark had been.

I flew to Amarillo and met my DEA partner, Joseph LaSalle, at the Amarillo airport. Because of the possible danger of the assignment, I was delighted my partner was a career DEA Agent.

It was very important to the secrecy of the assignment that the Trustee, Adolph Riddler, not know in advance of our coming before our arrival at his office.

Riddler had come under suspicion after a well-known Chinese mafia-type individual had been seen coming out of Riddler's office several times. Ah Kum Jianguo was supposed to be an informant for the DEA, but his recent activities had aroused suspicions that he may not be the "paragon of virtue" DEA had originally thought him to be. FBI background investigation had revealed him to be a member of a West Coast mafia-type gang known as "Dragon Rules" who resort to violence when anyone invades their territory. My job was to try and determine if Riddler's trusteeship was being used for drug smuggling to try and hide illegal income.

After meeting LaSalle, we headed for his favorite Amarillo restaurant. I certainly didn't object because it had been several hours since my last meal.

The Big Texan Steak Ranch is known to thousands of tourists and locals. According to some of our people at EOUST who had been in Amarillo, this restaurant was well-known for their offer that you ate free if you could finish their seventy-two ounce porterhouse, including all of the trimmings. Of course that included a huge Irish potato and likewise oversized salad. You had to finish it all.

I asked the waitress if anyone ever was able to win the free steak. She told me that NFL players and wrestlers were so successful they stopped offering it free.

I ordered a large hamburger steak with fries and salad. It was well worth the thirty minute wait it took to prepare it. While we were eating, we were entertained by a group who played and sang Western type ballads. Several couples got up and danced. The restaurant experience was a great way to begin my Amarillo adventure.

The next day Joseph and I went to the Trustee's office, located on the top floor of one of Amarillo's tallest buildings. I introduced Joseph as a member of our accounting staff and told Riddler we were there to conduct an inspection of his Trustee financial records. I presented him with a copy of the letter authorizing our inspection.

It was obvious to both Joseph and me that our presence upset the Trustee badly. He stammered that his accounting records were at his accountant's office which of course we didn't believe. I asked his accountant's name which Riddler refused to give me. Hoping to satisfy us he let us see the files on his Chapter 7 cases. We reviewed them and made notes, but there was nothing in them that particularly interested us. I asked him to give us a time and date when his financial records would be available but he refused to tell us anything. If he was trying to make us suspicious, he was doing a superb job.

That evening I reported our experience with Riddler to Director Callahan and LaSalle reported the same to his boss. The US Trustee office and the DEA office, both located in Lubbock, were notified, and we were directed to travel to Lubbock to get further instructions and to review information they had regarding Riddler's trusteeship that might be helpful.

The next morning Joseph and I traveled the 124 miles to Lubbock on Interstate 27. That highway is so flat and boring that I believe you could roll a bowling ball at the city limits of Amarillo and it would eventually end up in Lubbock. We went to the UST office first. The US Trustee had already obtained a court order, delivered to Riddler's bank, requiring production of copies of the checks and deposit slips I needed for my examination, and the bank promised the documents would be available in about a week. Next, Joseph and I went to his DEA office for a conference with his supervisor.

At the DEA office I was brought up-to-date on what they had and what they suspected. The informant was a Chinese immigrant named Ah Kum Jianguo living in McAllen Texas. He had been feeding bits and pieces of information to the DEA regarding the smuggling of illegal drugs across the border from Reynosa, Mexico.

The DEA chief authorized Joseph to go to McAllen to see if he could get Ah Kum Jianguo to reveal the identity of the border guard suspected in being part of the smuggling operation. He also suggested that I accompany Joseph in order that we impress Ah Kum Jianguo with our strength in numbers.

Off to McAllen, Texas we went. I tried not to let my nervousness show about going on a mission that had no connection with financial records. Joseph picked up on that right away. I was still not comfortable in his assurance that he was fully armed and knew how to protect me. I hope my desire to let him know that I was up to the challenge would overcome my fear. We were given the informant's secret codes for getting in touch with him, so that afternoon we flew to San Antonio and rented a car for our drive to McAllen. My instincts that told me I would regret this move later.

We met Ah Kum Jianguo in the back room of an old Chinese restaurant. Joseph had a list of all of the security guards at the McAllen crossing points and was in the process of discussing each name with the informant in hopes he would reveal the identity of the renegade border guard. About half way through the list the informant turned hostile. He had been eyeing me and tried to draw me into a conversation about what my role was, and I couldn't give him a satisfactory answer. He then refused to even speculate who the maverick border guard might be without absolute assurances from Joseph that he could go into the Witness-Protection program. Joseph didn't have the authority to grant his request. That is when it really turned nasty. Ah Kum Jianguo got up and left, leaving Joseph and me alone in a strange restaurant in a strange town.

We left in our car and got on the road leading back to San Antonio. It was late at night now and there was practically no traffic. About five miles out of McAllen, we both noticed a black SUV that had just pulled up right behind us. It was right on our bumper. Joseph sped up but the SUV continued and stayed right with us. Joseph sped up to more than ninety miles per hour but still the SUV hugged our bumper. Finally, on a long straight stretch, it pulled up beside us and a shot rang out. Joseph was hit and our car went out of control, rolling down a hill. I was thrown from the car and immediately afterwards our car hit a tree head-on and burst into flame. I could see the two armed men from the SUV surveying the scene to kill any survivors. I had somehow landed in a drainage ditch and was out of sight from anyone on the road so it was easy for our pursers to assume that both of us were killed in the fire that consumed the car. I was hurt and badly shook up but I was alive. The killers didn't stay around long because cars were now stopping to see what had happened. I had to get out of that ditch because there was no telling what kind of crawling creature might be in there with me. I didn't want to be found by anybody because I didn't know whom to trust. I was both mentally and physically exhausted. Soon I heard sirens and was able to limp to some cedar trees located far enough away from the main road that I would not be seen. Limping to the trees I was afraid of stepping on a rattler, but more afraid of anyone hunting for me. I passed the time until morning by trying to remember and recite Bible verses I had learned as a child. Otherwise, I spent a cold and miserable night.

The next morning I was able to half walk and half crawl to a farm house about a quarter of a mile away. The people were friendly and offered to feed me and treat my wounds, but I was in no condition to eat. All I wanted to do was to get away from McAllen Texas as soon as I could find a way to do that. They agreed to take me to a restaurant about five miles away. My side was hurting bad and I had difficulty breathing. I didn't dare try to get any medical care until I could get miles away from McAllen and the men who killed Joseph and who had tried to kill me.

At the restaurant I was able to catch a Trailways bus which took me to San Antonio. There, I had a uber driver take me to Kindred Hospital and to the emergency room. The driver had to help me out of the car into the facility, and once there, I passed out from the pain.

When I awoke, I was in a hospital room with tubes and wires running everywhere from my body. A pretty nurse came in and seeing I was awake, she took my blood pressure and temperature and went to get the physician who had been treating me. He came in and explained that I had three cracked ribs and wanted to know how I got them. I lied and told him I was in construction and I was painting a house in town and fell off the ladder. I don't know if he believed me or not, but as there hadn't been any notifications from local law enforcement about anyone fitting my description, the lie seemed to satisfy him. Later though the pretty nurse looked at my smooth hands and clean nails and whispered: "house painter my ass!" She winked at me and left me alone to ponder what was going to happen next.

The next day they let me use the phone to call Zack Callahan. He had already received word of the shooting and feared I had been killed. He immediately got in touch with Federal Marshals in San Antonio, and they came to guard my room with specific instructions that I was to receive no visitors. The one exception to the "No Visitor" rule was when Rebecca showed up. She had contacted Callahan a couple of days ago after not hearing from me for three days, and then when she learned I was in the hospital, she flew to San Antonio to be with me. I felt so relieved when I was able to finally hold her in my sore arms! She stayed with me two or three days until the doctor told her I was out of danger and then she returned to Washington.

I was in the hospital for two more weeks before they finally released me. The hospital had me registered under a fictitious name to protect me in case the McAllen hoods came looking for me. Fortunately, there was no news coverage article about the stranger who appeared from nowhere posing as a house painter to cover up his real identity. I caught the first plane to Washington not looking forward to the consequences of my ill-fated trip to Amarillo and McAllen, Texas.

CHAPTER 6

The Doghouse

Zack Callahan was furious. In Washington, bad news travels fast. In government, it travels at warp speed. The Attorney General, of course, had learned about my involvement in the Texas disaster and came down hard on Callahan. At first, he wanted Callahan to fire me, but Callahan saved my job by promising to discipline me severely. He was angry with me for disobedience, and angry at DEA for going outside the chain of command. That is a major offence in Civil Service, but only once it makes a supervisor look bad.

"You are a fool. You had no training at all in DEA matters, and you are being blamed for the DEA agent's death since he was trying to protect you. Furthermore, the DEA head in Lubbock told me he didn't even know you were going to McAllen, Texas."

Oh, so that's what this is all about. The DEA head trying to protect his rear end. I understood that.

After listening to Callahan rant and rave for thirty minutes, he told me I was grounded until he could decide what to do with me.

I felt crushed by Callahan's disappointment in me.

"I want you to review reports of other analyses for awhile. You can work from your home until I tell you different."

This was the low point of my entire career. I was really in the "Dog House." Feeling sorry for myself, I felt a kinship with Napoleon when he was banished to the island of St. Helena. I was determined though to maturely take the discipline and not become defensive or resentful.

A week after my exile to Helen, Rebecca came to my rescue. She knew I was disheartened about what happened on the Texas trip and she wanted to encourage me. That was hard because I blamed myself for what happened to Joseph LaSalle. He had a wife and two small children.

Rebecca and I decided to take a trip to Lubbock, Texas to visit with Joseph's family. This was a short, very expensive trip. His wife was very grateful for our visit. His children were sad but well-behaved. The family was receiving financial help through DEA. His wife told us she had always worried about Joseph's work because it was so dangerous. She did not appear to blame me for Joseph's death.

During our plane trip to Texas, Rebecca talked about our future. We had been dating for four years and she had finally lost her fear of marriage. Her dad and mother had an ugly divorce. Rebecca blamed it on her mother's alcoholism. Her dad was an attorney with the Internal Revenue Service and traveled a lot. Her mother's loneliness led her to the bottle. She resisted anyone trying to help. When things got intolerable, her Dad abandoned the family. Rebecca became mother and father to her two younger brothers. She never forgave her dad, and always feared that if she got married, it would turn out the same as her parent's marriage.

I was very much in love with Rebecca and wanted to marry her, but I didn't want to ask her during a plane trip. I wanted my proposal to be unique and unforgettable!

After we returned to Helen, I conjured up a plan. I convinced her to join me in a canoe trip down the Chattahoochee River. There is a rather significant part of the river that goes over some class 3 rapids. I purposely maneuvered the canoe over the rapids sideways where it would overturn and down we both went into the cold water. I figured this was as good a spot as any so when she came up for air, hanging on to me for "dear life," and then glaring at me and murmuring something like, "you meant to do that." I finally got up the courage to ask her right then and there to marry me, and to my utter surprise she said "Yes!"

We went and talked to the minister of the Baptist church I had been attending. I told him everything including some of the details of my disastrous trip to Texas. Rebecca also told him about her dysfunctional family, and her earlier hesitation about marriage. It turned out the minister was from my adopted hometown of Cookeville where my sister taught school. He didn't know any of my family, but it was nice to get to know him.

We planned our wedding and invited a few guests including some members of the church. My sister and her Bill were there, and to my surprise, so was Zack Callahan. Not a word about work or my recent troubles, but he did play smacky-lips with my bride at the reception. My best man was Eddie Cruise who had become my best friend and who had introduced me to

Rebecca years ago. We invited Rebecca's younger brothers and also both of Rebecca's parents. We didn't know what to expect from her parents. Having them present proved to be our most difficult moments. Her mother stayed intoxicated and her dad had to remove her from the ceremony. There was something good that came from this besides our marriage. Rebecca and her dad were able to reconcile. It was the first time I had seen her cry. Later she admitted the tears were tears of emotional relief after so many years of resentment.

We flew to Alaska for a week-long honeymoon. We stayed in a small motel near Denali National Park, and the following day we got on a park bus and enjoyed a tour of the park. We saw moose, deer, wolves, and caribou, but the most interesting and entertaining animals were the two grizzlies and their three cubs all playing together near a river. Of course, we didn't dare get up too close, but we enjoyed them from a distance. Another day we were able to do some fishing in the Kanai River where I caught two nice salmon.

While we were in Alaska, I bought a San Francisco newspaper as it was the only lower forty-eight states newspaper available. There was an interesting story about how a San Francisco attorney, named Dexter Freeman, had accused local bankruptcy court officials of corruption in their administration of bankruptcy cases. I wondered aloud if the EOUST might investigate the complaint.

All too soon we were back in Helen. We needed a place to live, a bit more sophisticated than my bachelor pad I had been living in. This was a huge step for us both. We found a great mountainside cabin near Helen, perfectly located on a creek that emptied into the Chattahoochee. It was located in the National Forest and was close to town, perfect for hiking and fishing. We both proudly went to the real estate closing and treasured the warranty deed to our new home.

Rebecca's law firm had offices in several large cities including Atlanta. She was able to get her firm to transfer her there. I figured if I could just get out of the exile situation I was in, we would be in tall cotton.

Two months later though nothing had changed. The Washington office was sending me inspection reports to review daily. Having been once exposed to the front line but now confined to reviewing reports, my daily work had become monotonous.

October turned into November and suddenly Thanksgiving was upon us. Rebecca tried to keep my spirits up, but it became a chore to get up in the morning. I thought about leaving the agency, but I really loved the work I was doing before my exile so I hung on to the hope that this too would pass. Then before we knew it, it was Christmas time. Rebecca did a great job of decorating the cabin and yard and even I enjoyed it. She got me a new fly-fishing outfit for Christmas and I got her a real ring. New Year's found us celebrating in Alpine Helen. The town locals and tourists danced in the streets to a German band from Atlanta. For the two hours of the celebration, no one was allowed to take a car through the main street because that had been shut down for the occasion. Later Rebecca and I wondered aloud what the New Year might hold for us.

At 8 a.m. on January 2nd, I got a call from Zack Callahan's assistant instructing me to come to Washington immediately.

Did this mean I might be returned to active duty? Fired?

I would soon find out.

CHAPTER 7

Special Assignment #37 – San Francisco

I arrived at EOUST promptly at 9 a.m. on Monday morning, both eager and wary to find out what fate awaited me.

"Good morning, Jeffrey. It's good to see you. You're looking well" were the first civil words Callahan had spoken to me in months. Maybe I was out of his dog house? "I want you to meet Wyatt Truman. He's the chief investigator for the UST in San Francisco."

Wyatt Truman was an imposing figure, towering over the two of us in his white Stetson and cowboy boots. He could have just as easily been named "Wyatt Earp" of TV Western fame.

Truman launched into a shocking story of malfeasances happening in the bankruptcy cases in the San Francisco area. He described what appeared to be a pattern of unjust enrichment by Bay area Trustees. He claimed to know of several cases where Trustees were keeping cases alive to generate for themselves extra fees. He alleged there were several Trustees engaged in such behavior. All of these cases were being serviced by the same bankruptcy judge in Oakland. A Trustee by the name of

Leon Quirk was suspected by Truman to be the ring-leader of the scheme.

The main thrust of Truman's concerns was that The San Francisco Chapter 7 Trustees were out of control because they were completely unsupervised and unaccountable. Their bank account records had never been audited. If true, a major part of the responsibility for this failure in administration had to fall here at the EOUST. Besides the possibility of cheating creditors of potentially millions of dollars they might be entitled to, a scam of this nature would be a source of scandal and embarrassment to the entire national bankruptcy program.

Truman said that he had brought this situation to the attention of his boss, San Francisco US Trustee Tony Santos, and had suggested conducting audits or examinations of all Chapter 7 Trustees. He proposed setting up a system where these Trustees would be supervised and held accountable in accordance with Departmental Regulations.

Santos reacted by asking, "Who else knows about this?"

"No one. Not yet. Just you."

"Good, Truman. Keep it between just the two of us for now. It's important to the security of this office and for the safety of your family that we keep a lid on this for now. You never know what could happen if the wrong people found out."

Santos then explained the cost of implementing what Truman was suggesting was way beyond what his budget could justify; further, the office could not spare Truman to implement the suggested procedures himself.

As Truman, like all key employees of the office, served at the pleasure of the US Trustee, he couldn't insist, but after being sent to Washington for his annual in-house training and review exercises, Truman was able to get Director Callahan to listen to his concerns.

Zack Callahan had told me months before, he had been hearing bits and pieces of possible irregularities involving bankruptcy cases in the Bay area for the eight years he had been the EOUST Director. The name "Leon Quirk" rang an unpleasant bell in the Director's head, although he couldn't recall the specifics.

"I seem to recall complaints about Quirk from a letter I received from a debtor named Silvertongue, Silverspoon or Silversomething, and I told Tony Santos to check the complaint out and deal with it. He told me later that he had taken care of it."

"I never heard of a name anything like that," piped up Truman." ....and stuff like that is my job. I can't stand being left out of the loop on something that important."

Truman added: "If you gentlemen don't have anything else, I really have to get going. I'm due in my class downstairs, and I don't want to arouse any suspicions. Santos can be a very scary guy. Here's my phone number if you need it."

He left quickly after Callahan thanked him for his good work and the risk he took by talking to us.

So, Callahan and I were alone in the room, finally.

After an awkward moment, we got down to the elephant in the room; the Texas matter.

"The people who tried to kill you down there were apparently hit men who disappeared right after they got Joseph LaSalle and the attempt on your life. The bank sent us all of the documents you asked for on Riddler. I was going to assign you to complete what you started, but the San Francisco matter is too important. I'll put you on the Texas case later."

"Jeff, you know you were wrong not to call me when you said you would before anyone assigned you to any DEA action, but the main thing is that you're ok. That was an awful experience you had down there, and I feel really bad about what happened to LaSalle. You and I have been close ever since you arrived here, and I would never have forgiven myself if you had been killed or permanently disabled in that assassination attempt."

WOW! I guessed I was now out of Callahan's doghouse.

That was the end of the subject and we never discussed it again.

Callahan told me he had spoken to the Attorney General about problems in the San Francisco area on more than one occasion, and was told to keep an eye on the happenings in that office and to "keep me posted." That's bureaucrat language for "I better not hear about this again," meaning the complaints about no corrective action was ever taken.

The Attorney General instructed Callahan to get his best investigator to San Francisco to try to uncover any truth to the suspicions, and that is when Callahan instructed me to come to Washington. I was flattered that I was so well thought of, particularly after the Texas trip disaster.

Callahan informed me that I was being sent to San Francisco on Special Assignment #37. The term "Special Assignment" meant that an agent was to report only to the Director. The scope of my assignment was to conduct a thorough examination of Trustee Quirk's financial records.

"Director, what if US Trustee Santos refuses to let me conduct the examination?"

"Just remember that I am your boss, not Tony Santos. I'll send him a letter to that effect and he can call me if there are any questions."

The really good news I received from Callahan was that my good friend, Eddie Cruise, was being transferred to San Francisco and that he would be working on any criminal elements involved in the case.

It was clear that this situation was a lot broader and deeper than Trustee Quirk; it involved the integrity of the entire bankruptcy system in San Francisco.

I turned to leave. Just as I got to the door, he called me. "Allan!" I turned and look at him. "Don't mess this up!"

I knew he meant it.

I had dinner that night with Eddie and his wife Christa. They were both surprised at Eddie's transfer but were determined to make the most of it. We had worked well together on the New Jersey case, so this part of our new assignments appealed to both of us.

But Christa wasn't thrilled about moving their two small children 3,000 miles away. It meant finding a new house and neighborhood, away from family and friends, but she said she was determined to see it through. FBI life was the one they had chosen, and transfers were a price that had to be paid to be a Special Agent in the world's most famous investigative organization.

My assignment presented me with a dilemma I now had to face. There was no telling how long this assignment was going to last. It might mean I would be separated from my wife for the length of my assignment with the small consolation that I could fly home twice a month over the weekend. Well, at least that was something.

I flew home to pack and told Rebecca of my assignment, and she wasn't excited about the separation either. But she was always one to put a positive spin on challenges that seemingly had no satisfactory solution. Her law firm had an office in San Jose, only a few miles to the south of San Francisco and she would check to see if they could temporarily transfer her to that location.

It took me seven hours to get to San Francisco. After changing planes in Houston and again in Denver, I finally arrived around midnight, San Francisco time. Exhausted from having been on the move for hours, I crashed in bed at the airport motel.

The next morning, I got an Uber driver to take me to a previously selected motel on Van Ness Avenue. Our office chose that location because of its large desk and working space in the rooms which would enable me to keep my work away from curious eyes.

This was Saturday and so after resting up, I decided to tour part of the city. I took a trolley ride into the heart of Chinatown and ate some very good oriental food. Then, after walking for several hours and marveling at the beauty of the city I had worked up quite an appetite, so I took another trolley to Fisherman's Wharf. The crab legs were sensational for this southern boy!

On the way back to my living quarters I decided to walk and find the Federal Building where I would be going tomorrow. I was repeatedly confronted along the way by homeless people who were living on the streets. I wondered about them; why were they homeless, and who cared about them?

Wyatt Truman had already returned to San Francisco, and when I arrived at the office, we were to act as though we had just met. We thought it important to keep his meeting with Callahan a secret.

My biggest concern was that this whole thing could get awkward in a hurry. What if Santos doesn't let me into his office? What if he discovers his chief investigator went behind his back to set up my being assigned here? What if Santos is somehow involved in this mystery? I had been granted leave out of Callahan's doghouse, and I was determined to make sure this assignment begins the way Callahan intended.

Those questions and more to come would have to be faced. For now, I was worn out from all the walking and it was time to go to bed.

CHAPTER 8

The Embezzler

"Jeffrey Allan, I'm Tony Santos. Zack Callahan told me you would be here this morning. Glad you're here. Welcome to San Francisco!"

At first, I was pleasantly surprised by the warm welcome I got, but then my "Bunk-O-Meter" went off, reminding me that a political animal like Santos doesn't get to where he's at by snipping at the heels of those who might be able to negatively affect his career.

Santos was a short and heavy set man with hair parted in the middle and a mustache. He introduced me to Wyatt Truman who pretended like we had just met. Wyatt led me to a table in the middle of the typing pool, explaining they didn't have any empty offices at the moment. I told him that was ok because I would be doing most of my work from my motel room.

I was assigned a departmental automobile, but with strict instructions, it could be used for Trustee business only. It had to be parked there at the headquarters every evening, requiring me to get back to my motel the best way I could. I was told the reason for this was because the insurance company threatened to increase the premiums on any car taken to a San Francisco motel. Their restriction seemed silly. Wyatt told me he would take me to my room every day after we finished our work.

I drove over to Oakland to meet with Bankruptcy Trustee Leon Quirk. Wyatt Truman had told his contact in the US Attorney's office that I would probably need help in getting the banks to make copies of deposit and check documents. I was given a name to call.

Quirk was about six foot seven inches tall and as skinny as a rail. My mind flashed an image of Quirk and Santos standing together, reminiscent of the old Mutt and Jeff cartoons.

I suspected someone had tipped Quirk off that I was on my way to meet him. He refused to let me see any of his financial records. He claimed that the bankruptcy judge told him that we needed a court order to see them. That wasn't true, but it was easier to get the court order than to butt heads with Quirk at this early stage.

The next morning, I got the order from the Federal District Court, thanks to Wyatt Truman and his many contacts in the Federal court system. I immediately began to create a spreadsheet of Quirk's banking. It soon became evident that Quirk's in-house records didn't match the records from the bank. The bank documents revealed a number of transactions involving a winery named "Shebrooke" and several more that involved an organization identified as "Outfront, Inc." Neither of these organizations was identified in the court records of having any standing in bankruptcy matters or being a party in any bankruptcy case.

Even more revealing, none of the transactions of "Shebrooke" or "Outfront, Inc." were included in the Trustee's financial reports to the Bankruptcy Court. After spending nearly a month of digging through banking, court and county records, my analysis revealed more than $5,000,000 of illegal payments from the Bankruptcy bank account to Shebrooke. My investigation also revealed the owner of Shebrooke to be none other than Leon Quirk. He had purchased the winery at a Bankruptcy auction. No wonder Quirk didn't want anyone digging around in his records.

There were no court orders for the payments to Shebrooke. Checks were written and disbursed with no apparent court authorization. My spreadsheets revealed that funds used to make the disbursements to Shebrooke came from the sale at auction of properties of bankrupt debtors whose properties had been taken over by the Bankruptcy Court, and administered by Quirk.

Of course, this meant that the creditors of these bankrupted cases didn't get nearly as much money as they were entitled to because a big portion of those funds went illegally to Shebrooke and then to Quirk.

Further investigation revealed that the closing reports on cases were filed with the bankruptcy court without the inclusion of the payments made to Shebrooke. This was clearly Bankruptcy Fraud, punishable by long prison terms. Practically, no creditor objected at the closing of the relevant cases because they were unaware of the Shebrooke payments. Quirk used the Trustee's bank account like it was his own personal bank account.

In the evenings I met with Truman and brought him up to date with what my day's findings were. We both remembered Callahan's instructions to not reveal to Santos the results of my findings.

Wyatt Truman told me that an attorney by the name of Dexter Freeman, who represented several debtors, repeatedly objected to the handling of his client's cases by the Court. Freeman's constant challenges had become a headache to the US Trustee. Santos decided to silence Freeman by filing "Motions to Dismiss" on every case challenged by Freeman, even though Santos was not a party to the action. The Court had accepted the motions. This was highly unusual.

About half way through my examination, it became apparent to me that Quirk suspected that I had discovered his embezzlement. He was clearly under pressure in the office. He was late, missing appointments, screaming at his employees, and appeared on several occasions to be hung over. One particular evening, just before closing time, I took a handful of files from my desk, down the stairs to return them to the file room located in the basement. A young, attractive brunette followed me to the file room, attempted to rub up against me, and whispered that she would love to buy me a drink after the office closed. That sort of thing just didn't happen to me….ever….I was sure the woman's invitation was a not-so-subtle way Quirk had in trying to catch me in a trap.

After three weeks of each of us living alone, Rebecca was able to join me in San Francisco. Her law firm's office in San Jose arranged it. Drive time was about an hour each way, but the case she was assigned to was being tried in the Federal District

Court in San Francisco. We were in the same building. What a blessing that was.

We worked long hours during the week, but had great weekends together. We tried to do something different each weekend. From the beaches across Golden State Bridge, the Redwoods at the Armstrong Natural Reserve, Pebble Beach to the South. Having two decent salaries we were able to afford the great seafood and oriental eating places in "Frisco." Our favorite place was brunch at the Cliff House watching the playful seals stacked on top of each other. Returning to work on Mondays was not always easy, but we were both committed to be good stewards of our positions.

Quirk's fraudulent banking practices regarding "Outfront, Inc." were not going to be as easy to decode as Shebrooke's had been. In that case, there was a paper trail which was easy to follow through the bank records, case files, and real estate deeds. The embezzled funds originated from the sale of existing bankruptcy case properties and were paid out to Shebrooke and then paid from Shebrooke to Quirk. But the "Outfront, Inc." matter was different. There apparently were no existing bankruptcy cases relative to the incoming Outfront funds which were coming in from a yet unknown source. Like the New Jersey case, payments made to Outfront were equal in amounts to the deposits coming into the account. Sometimes there were several checks adding up to a particular deposit that had been made, and sometimes several deposits were added together to make up a single check to Outfront, probably in an attempt to cover up the exact total of the transfers. Investigation revealed these incoming funds were coming from a Swiss bank, and disbursed several days later to Outfront. The bank Outfront was using was in the Cayman Islands. So, Quirk's bank account was being used to launder funds to cover up something. The question was, "What was he trying to hide?"

The Outfront issues would have to wait until I completed the embezzlement case against Quirk. I had enough evidence on Quirk on just the Shebrooke transactions to send him to prison for years. Callahan and I discussed the case thoroughly. He told me to complete my report, keep my work secure, and not to say a word to Santos or anyone else.

"Jeffrey, this looks like the largest single case of Bankruptcy fraud ever discovered. I need you to be in DC on Monday morning to meet with the Attorney General and me. Don't tell anyone but Rebecca, and by the way, you can bring her along to the Agency. I think you will be here about three days. Just make sure you secure your files and documents. Don't leave anything in your motel room. These guys could be dangerous."

I was delighted not to have to leave her alone in San Francisco. She was still involved in the case she was sent out here on, but she was able to arrange for someone to cover for her for a few days.

When I got to the EOUST, Callahan had just gotten off the phone with an apoplectic Tony Santos. Santos found out somehow that I had received a lot of my help and information from Wyatt Truman, and Santos fired him on the spot. He used some excuse about a questionable tax return Wyatt had filed with the IRS years earlier, before being assigned to the US Trustee's office. Later I learned that Santos had known about the tax return when

Wyatt came to work there. Wyatt had an exemplary work record, and Santos used that tax return as an excuse to fire him.

I felt bad for Wyatt because he had been such a big help to my investigation, at some considerable risk, and had proven himself to be a man of integrity.

Before leaving to return to San Francisco, I called Wyatt, with Director Callahan's permission.

"Hey, Wyatt, I'm so sorry that you got fired over this. It's not right."

"Well, my conflicts with Santos had been intensifying for some time, and it had to come to a head eventually. I've been saving a lot of my paycheck so my wife and I will be all right. Actually, my parents left me their cattle ranch in Montana and I've been leasing it out, but the lease just expired, so we won't be homeless like all those folks in San Francisco. They're the ones who really need a job."

"Wyatt, we'd like to have you as a consultant from time to time. I've talked to Director Callahan and he has approved this. Maybe we can talk about this later. In any case, I'd like to stay in touch with you."

"Sure, great. Tell Zack Callahan I appreciate him."

Overall, my two-day meetings with the Attorney General went well. He was an experienced criminal lawyer. We plotted our strategy and I became comfortable with what he was recommending. I was told a United States Marshall was being assigned to watch Leon Quirk to make sure he wasn't planning to escape on a flight overseas.

Afterwards, Rebecca and I left for our return flight to San Francisco.

When we got to our motel room, we discovered that someone had broken in and "tossed" our room. It was clear to the cops the perpetrators were looking for something specific. I was so thankful I had been able to get Rebecca to come with me. When word of the break-in reached the Attorney General, he assigned another US Marshall to watch and protect Rebecca and me.

I spent the next morning preparing to meet with the Grand Jury. Rebecca took another day off and met with a real estate lady to try and find us a condo we could rent rather that the motel room.

The following day I met with the US Attorney's staff in San Francisco. At that meeting were Trustee Quirk and his attorney, Peter Seabolt. I sat and listened intently while Seabolt explained his client's willingness to cooperate with the Feds in exchange for a more lenient sentence on the embezzlement charge. He promised full cooperation in exchange for a sentence of no more than three years in a minimum security prison close to San Francisco. In exchange, Seabolt promised a list of names, including US government officials who were either heavily involved or complicit, regarding the large-scale bankruptcy corruption that was happening in the San Francisco area.

Plea Agreement or not, Leon Quirk was going down.

CHAPTER 9

Crooks in Cahoots

Assistant US Attorney Larry Albright eyeballed Seabolt with his best poker-faced lie.

"Look, Peter, you know that I can't give you any protective custody deal until we know what your client has to offer, and even then we have to get the Attorney General's approval. We need something real here. You've been around the block. You know that."

Quirk was fidgeting and looked real nervous, just where Albright wanted him. Quirk knew he shouldn't have been in this meeting, and Seabolt knew he had made a negotiating mistake. He could have done better if he had left Quirk in the other room.

Quirk's hands and face were sweating, and it wasn't from the room temperature. He spoke up.

"I've got some real big names, much bigger than you are expecting, but I'm not giving you guys nothing without a guarantee. I could get killed."

Albright pounced. "You should have thought of that before you betrayed the trust you were given, Leon. We know who you're protecting. We just don't have all the proof yet."

"If you guys know so much, then why don't you make some arrests?" said Seabolt, trying to get the heat off him and his client.

"So give us some names and what else you've got and I'll do my best to get the Attorney General to give you an answer real quick." The fear in Quirk's face told Albright he held all the cards.

"Screw you guys! Let's get out of here, Peter. Maybe we'll go to the Attorney General ourselves."

As they had no documents with them, it was easy for Peter Seabolt and a stressed out Leon Quirk to just get up and leave. The poker game had begun. First meetings usually went like this, both sides playing hardball.

I was new to these kinds of meetings between the accused and the accuser. There was so much on the line for the accused, but it seemed to me that it would not be a good idea to string Quirk along too long.

The next day I got a call from Eddie Cruise with his new address and phone number in the Bay area. He had been officially designated the "Lead Agent" on the case now known as "SFRUPT", to include any bankruptcy fraud uncovered by my examinations. I met him at his office, and we reviewed the files I had put together on Quirk. He agreed with my thinking that if the main players were above Quirk and if they were who I thought them to be, we had better move quickly. He would check with the Special Agent in Charge (SAC) of the San Francisco office to see if he could expedite a protective agreement for Quirk.

That night Rebecca and I had dinner with Eddie and his wife at John's Grill. Behind us on the wall were pictures of Joe DiMaggio, mostly in his Yankee baseball uniform, and a couple of him with Marilyn Monroe. We reminisced about our college days and our wedding ceremonies. Seems like that's a topic most women like to talk about, and it's much better than two guys talking shop all the time. An important theme in Eddie's and my training had been to not discuss our cases in public. During World War II there was an important warning given to all soldiers in basic training: "Loose lips sink ships." There had been several cases of overheard conversations and careless talk that led to several allied disasters, including several that almost tipped the enemy off about the Normandy invasion.

Eddie and I were awaiting our instructions on how we were to proceed on the Quirk plea offer.

In the meantime, local newspapers had begun a daily series of articles about Leon Quirk, outlining the embezzlement charges with information they had gathered from their sources. This led to a string of letters to the newspapers and to the US Trustee's office from potential victims of bankruptcy fraud. Debtors were alleging fraudulent seizure and conversion of their assets, while creditors were accusing Trustees of withholding funds they were entitled to from bankrupt estates. They all demanded justice.

I was just about ready to leave the office for the weekend. My phone rang. It was Eddie.

"Have you ever heard of an attorney named Dexter Freeman?" I told him that the mention of that name brought on a headache to the US Trustee. Freeman was constantly calling the UST office, accusing employees of complicity for overlooking bankruptcy fraud.

Eddie told me that Freeman had a client who alleged to have gotten scammed by Leon Quirk. The client wanted to have an immediate meeting with Eddie and "the guy who broke the Leon Quirk case" so that he could present evidence of corruption in the system.

The thought crossed my mind that I could be venturing into the same sort of government hot water that got me in trouble in Texas.

The following Monday morning Freeman introduced me to his client, Rodney Silvertongue. We sat and listened to what he had to say.

"I've been producing wine for over twenty years. About five years ago, making money became more difficult because of the entry into the business of several new producers. A couple of my suppliers who were also suppliers to my competitors loaned me money against future production. Then we had a fire which wiped out a large part of my vineyard. This drastically affected production for a couple of years, and I fell behind in my payments on my loan. Those suppliers pressured me for payments to the extent of forcing me to file for Chapter 11 of the Bankruptcy statute, which would enable me to hold off my creditors and still let me stay in business."

"Eight months later I get this letter from the Bankruptcy Court, advising me that my case had been converted to a Chapter 7 case, which called for immediate liquidation of my assets and distribution of any money from the sale of my assets to my creditors. Before I received that letter, I had no idea this was taking place and that my business was being taken from me. That's when I went to Dexter Freeman."

Attorney Freeman then took over the conversation.

"I don't usually handle bankruptcy cases, but Rodney's case intrigued me because of rumors I had been hearing from other people who claimed to have gotten screwed in bankruptcy. It looked like he had been railroaded by the Court, and the attorney he had gone to on the bankruptcy matter should have protected him."

I asked who his previous attorney was. "Peter Seabolt."

Of course, we remembered Seabolt. How could we forget our previous meeting with him and embezzler Leon Quirk in Eddie's office?

Freeman continued by describing Seabolt's actions during the time Silvertongue's vineyard was under the jurisdiction of the bankruptcy court. Charges of incompetence or malpractice were among the tamer descriptions used to describe his services to Silvertongue. Freeman said the purpose of our meeting today was due to his inability to get any results from his previous complaints to US Trustee Tony Santos, and he hoped that what he had told was sufficient to warrant a complete investigation.

At this point, Silvertongue left, leaving the three of us to discuss a possible plan of action.

"I have five other clients with the same story, all of whom were previous clients of Peter Seabolt. I got so frustrated that I went to *The Chronicle* a few months ago, and told their investigative reporter the story. They published it, but after publishing one or two more similar articles, the story just died."

"I believe Santos and supervising Bankruptcy Judge Sidney Witherspoon are in cahoots, but I don't have any evidence; only a pattern of behavior. Now tell me, what do you guys think is going on? Do you think Quirk is a player in this?"

Eddie spoke up. "We can't really comment on that at this time. I will tell you we are looking into it."

"Tell us more about Mr. Silvertongue, if you would, please. He seems like a nice man, but he's had some tough luck, and he's made some questionable business decisions along the way, or he's gotten messed up with some less than decent guys."

"And I've got to ask you about that last name of his. Silvertongue? Don't think I've ever run into that name before."

"It's Cherokee Indian. His people originally came from North Carolina. He told me his ancestors were moved to Oklahoma in 1837 trudging along on the 'Trail of Tears' we've heard so much about. He was given a basketball scholarship to Oklahoma State and graduated with a degree in business. In my opinion, though, he is a classic example of someone having too much education and not enough common sense."

"In spite of his shortcomings, he didn't deserve what happened to him. I don't think what happened to him in the Bankruptcy Court could have happened without there being a conspiracy of two or more people connected with the Court."

I was careful not to let on that the vineyard in question was probably the vineyard bought by prior Bankruptcy Trustee Leon

Quirk as auctioned off on the Oakland courthouse steps. Eddie told Freeman that he appreciated the frankness of both him and his client, and told him we would investigate his concerns.

After Freeman left, Eddie and I were in complete agreement that there was coming together bits and pieces of evidence and information indicating a possible "stink bomb" within the Bay area bankruptcy system. That bomb would not just smell bad; it would taint the entire United States Bankruptcy System for many years.

Still waiting from word from Washington regarding Quirk's plea offer, and needing some work to justify my continued stay here, I asked Washington to send me copies of the bank documents of checks and deposits regarding the Amarillo case so I would have something to work on. To my surprise, upon looking at those documents I found the same deposit sources and disbursement locations I had found in my Leon Quirk investigation.

WOW!

Deposits were coming from a Swiss bank account, and withdrawals were going to a bank in the Cayman Islands. The M.O. was the same as Quirk's; the total of the deposits were equal in amount to the total of the withdrawals, but the individual items deposited in the Trust account were never identical to any item of withdrawal. I showed what I found to Eddie and he agreed with my analysis; it looked suspiciously like this tied in with Leon Quirk's maverick transactions.

Now we had two unanswered questions that we had to solve.

"How high up does these systematic frauds go in the Bay area?"

"What's the common thread of trusteeships in Amarillo, Texas, and San Francisco, California"?

CHAPTER 10

Dragon Rules

W orking with people in the legal profession is mostly enjoyable, but lawyers who work in government can be a pain in the butt, mostly because they feel their time is more valuable than anyone else's. There are exceptions to this; Zack Callahan is a notable exception, but Callahan is of a rare breed because he doesn't try to impress others with his importance.

I had been told by Assistant US Attorney Albright's secretary that he wanted to see me in his office at 8:30 a.m. sharp, presumably to discuss the Quirk demand for protective custody. Eddie had already told me that he had a meeting yesterday with Albright.

By arriving ten minutes early, as was my custom, I was attempting to show respect to the official I was meeting with. I was extremely anxious about Quirk being placed under protection of the United States Government without further delay.

At about 9:30 a.m. I walked down the hall to the men's room, and returned about ten minutes later. Naturally, Larry Albright was in the room, waiting for me.

"You're late, and I have a busy day, so let's get on with this, shall we?"

Albright continued. "Quirk wants us to pick him up at his home at nine tomorrow night. He gave me specific instructions on how we were to approach his home so that he could be sure it was us and not someone trying to hurt him."

I spoke up. "Why don't we quit fooling around and let's go get him now? He could be in some real danger if there is someone out there who suspects he wants to talk to us."

"Let me remind you that I'm the lead attorney in this office and I do this for a living. You're just the bean counter. This is my case, in case you forgot. I'm busy with a trial today and tomorrow, so tomorrow night will have to do. FBI agent Cruise will go with us."

The following evening around 8:30, Eddie and I headed for Quirk's home. Albright decided he was just too busy to make the trip with us. On the way there, Eddie and I talked about information we needed from Quirk, and just which one of us should be asking which question. We noticed a couple of emergency vehicles passing us as we got close, but we didn't pay much attention.

The residence was located in a swanky neighborhood filled with old, well-kept houses, and streets lined with oak trees. His street was adjacent to the San Francisco Golf Club near downtown Daly City. It looked like the area where people lived who weren't "on the way up." They were already there.

When we got to the address we were looking for, the driveway was clogged with those same emergency vehicles that had passed us. Cops were directing traffic, and tried to move us on along, but we parked down the street and attempted to approach the house. A police officer blocked the way. Eddie showed his badge and was allowed to enter but since I didn't have a badge they wouldn't let me follow him. I remembered I was just a "bean counter."

An hour later, Eddie came out with the news that Quirk had two bullets in his head, the tradecraft of a professional hit. The crime lab was already at the scene, but Eddie guessed there wouldn't be any clues left by the assassin(s).

Eddie did get permission for us to have unlimited access to the house. Quirk had been divorced for several years and lived by himself. The supervising police captain told us he would have the house guarded for as long as we needed it to be. We held our reports to our superiors until the next morning due to the late hour.

The next morning we began our inspection of Quirk's home office. We found where his laptop should have been but was nowhere to be seen. Papers and files were scattered everywhere. Whoever had done this knew what Quirk's role was and was trying to destroy any evidence.

Eddie called Quirk's attorney, Peter Seabolt, who told us he had just found out about his client's murder. He claimed to be in shock.

I passed Eddie a note and asked him to ask Seabolt when he had last seen Quirk.

"I had him in my office late yesterday afternoon. We were going over some paperwork."

"I don't have anything that can help you guys. He never told me the names of who he was giving up."

Eddie interrupted Seabolt. "How come you weren't here last night to meet with us? Isn't it customary that attorneys meet with their clients for such an important meeting as the one we had scheduled with him? You and he both knew our intention was to hear what he was going to give us, and then we would arrest him and place him into protective custody."

"Quirk felt that if his house was being watched, and they saw he was having a late-night meeting with his attorney, this might place him in immediate danger. I told him I needed to be there, but he insisted that I stay away."

Eddie tried to schedule another meeting with Seabolt.

"I don't have my schedule handy, but I don't think I can do it this week."

We searched the house looking for anything that might help us. I found, in his closet, crumpled up in one of his shirt pockets, a piece of paper with the name of Zhang Zhimin in Quirk's handwriting on it. That was it. Just the name, probably Chinese. No phone number; no address. Eddie called his office to get a name search started in the vast FBI Identification Division. We found some personal bank statements, but that was it. Whoever had broken into the house and carried out the assassination did a thorough job and had removed anything that looked like evidence. The crime lab returned while we were there and went back to work to try and uncover any prints, hairs, or anything else.

Just as we were ready to leave, Quirk's house phone rang. Eddie answered it and several times I heard him say, "Now who is this?"

"What was your relationship to Quirk."

"Please tell me your name so we can help you."

No response from the other side. The caller hung up without answering any of Eddie's questions. Eddie told me the call sounded like a young woman in distress. She wouldn't give her name.

When we returned from lunch, Eddie heard from the FBI's Identification Division. They had researched the name Zhang Zhimin and found he had an extensive criminal record. He was a member of a Chinese mafia-type gang known as "Dragon Rules," headquartered in Chinatown in San Francisco. They had criminal activities all over the orient. The organization was known for trafficking young girls from Thailand for prostitution. From there, they branched out into the illegal importing of food, mostly seafood, without having to pay customs tax. They then advanced to the sale and distribution of illegal drugs. They didn't care whom they sold to, and as a result, many of these drugs found their way into San Francisco area schools.

Zhimin had served time in San Quinton twice on State charges stemming from possession to the distributing of illegal substances. He was also suspected in a number of unsolved murders in and around the Bay area. The big question for us was, what was Zhimin's name doing in Quirk's possession? This was but another indication that there may be more to this Bankruptcy mess than the embezzlement of funds.

This was beginning to sound like my ill-fated Texas case, and the involvement of the missing Chinese "informer." I told Eddie about it and gave him the name of Ah Kum Jianguo, and Eddie called that name into the FBI ID division. About fifteen minutes later, they called back and said their records did not produce a match. Eddie surmised that he was probably just another illegal immigrant. I wasn't so sure. My instincts told me there were too many similarities between Amarillo and San Francisco.

We began looking into Quirk's bankruptcy files. All of Trustee Quirk's cases had been re-assigned by Bankruptcy Judge Witherspoon to San Francisco attorney, Judith Quarles. We called the FBI office and the EOUST in DC to get her bio, and then made a quick stop at the US District Court to obtain a warrant to search her files, should she prove uncooperative.

At the Bankruptcy Court, we were able to get a peek at some of her previously assigned cases, and I had no recognition of any of her cases of anyone lodging complaints.

Eddie tried to set up a face-to-face meeting but she said her schedule wouldn't allow for a meeting anytime this week. So, we conducted an interview by telephone. Her demeanor showed her to be a pleasant young woman, professional and friendly, but somewhat standoffish. Eddie and I both picked up on the mixed feeling she gave us.

Because of my experience in dealing with people in a more normal environment, I liked to put the person at ease, whereas my Crime Buster buddy wanted to go right after what we came for. It was sort of a "good cop, bad cop" approach. I think it made us more effective in dealing with a wide variety of people and issues.

Eddie began the questioning. "Ms. Quarles, we are looking into cases that were assigned to you which had previously been assigned to Leon Quirk. Have you noticed anything odd or out of the ordinary in any of those cases or in Quirk's files?"

"No, not really. I haven't had much of a chance yet to thoroughly review them."

"Do you know why they were assigned to you?"

"No."

I spoke up. "Ms. Quarles, at some point I'm probably going to be assigned the job of reviewing your financial records. Will you have any problem with that?"

"No. No problem at all."

After she hung up, Eddie told me he was glad we had that interview on the telephone and had heard her telephone voice because he was now 90 percent certain she was the one he had heard on the telephone the day after Quirk had been killed.

CHAPTER 11

A Trustee Very Close To Quirk(y)

I'm going to get this out of the way before I go any further. ALL Trustees are a bit odd, in my opinion, and that comes from a man who loves to analyze what makes up debits and credits. That, however, is not the world of Bankruptcy Trustees. They deal with people who, on the one hand, probably have lost all or nearly all of their money and stuff they had bought on credit and didn't or couldn't pay for them; people who probably made bad decisions, and are facing ruin of their reputations.

On the other side are merchants and lenders who feel they have been taken advantage of financially, and want some or all of their money or merchandise back from the people sitting across the table from them.

The Trustee has to be the referee of the wrestling match in accordance with the rules which most people don't understand. The process can take months or in some cases years, and makes most of the participants more than a little crazy.

Back in our living quarters, Rebecca handed me a stack of messages Alice, the receptionist at the US Trustee's office, had taken and phoned in to her. There were six messages from Callahan. Which glass of poison should I read first? I chose the predictable comfort of the shower over the surefire firing squad of Callahan's messages. Callahan would have to wait.

"Don't do a thing on the Quirk murder until you and I talk."

"Where the hell are you? Call me the second you get this."

"You had better be lying in another ditch somewhere."

"The AG wants a report on Quirk's death now. He heard the news tonight on his television. ON HIS TELEVISION!"

Those were the milder ones, but that was the flavor. The relevant directive for me was the last message. "Call my secretary whenever you get this message and I'm going to assign six new cases I want you to start on tomorrow morning."

So, I concluded in my lightning fast mind that I wasn't being fired. Rebecca and I splurged and drank a glass of wine in mock celebration.

The six cases I was assigned all involved Trustees with numerous complaints filed against them; two in San Francisco, one in Santa Rosa, and three in Oakland. About half of the complaints had originated from Attorney Dexter Freeman.

It took me two months to complete my audits. Most of my analysis work was done in the respective offices of the Trustees, but my reports were written after my field work in each case was completed because I didn't want to risk prying eyes to see what had been uncovered. I found it was much more secure for me to write my reports at the desk in our motel room, even though Rebecca had suggested that I write my reports in the US Trustee office cubbyhole I had been assigned in order to take advantage of secretarial help. I tried that, but I caught someone reading my notes and papers while I was at lunch one day, so I moved my final work on each audit to the makeshift area in our motel room I had designated as my office space.

After the murders of Leon Quirk and Joseph LaSalle, it was nice to turn to regular Forensic investigations with plain Vanilla crooks. In four of the six cases, there was evidence of very clumsy bankruptcy embezzlement attempts. All four subsequently pleaded guilty in order to avoid a trial.

The most important discovery was what wasn't there. Thorough examination of all six cases revealed no unrelated deposits or withdrawals, so there was no apparent connection of the six cases to the Quirk or Amarillo cases.

Callahan was pleased. "Good job on those cases, Jeffrey. You're going to make a decent investigator yet. You saved the taxpayers a ton of money with those guilty pleas."

"You know, most crooks are lazy. I guess that's why they try shortcuts to making a living. They're smart enough to find a way around the safeguards that have been set up and when they find a scheme that works, they use it over and over again thinking they won't get caught. The pattern of dishonesty becomes like their trademark or a badge of honor. They continue to use it because they seem to think we're too stupid to catch them."

"Now you can get back to Dexter Freeman. I've had several calls from him wanting to know how to get in touch with you. I told him you were out of town working on a case. I didn't give him your phone number. It's up to you if you want him to have it. Why don't you go meet with him? I think everyone in the UST office there believes him to be some kind of nut job. He didn't sound like that to me. Find out about his client Silvertongue too, and his vineyard. Sounds like something fishy is going on with that."

Dexter Freeman and I met for dinner. Monday nights are traditionally not a big night for the restaurant business, but someone forgot to tell the restaurants in Little Italy that because our restaurant was crowded. Dexter spoke Italian, and he ordered for me the spaghetti and meatballs which was good, but I should have brought a handful of relatives with me to finish it all.

Getting to know people is an easy part of my job, because most people like to talk about their favorite subject....themselves. However, this is often only a part of a person's character. This lawyer was no exception. Obviously, a silver spoon was a regular part of his table setting. He had gone to Harrow in London for his "academic preparatory work." Five generations had attended and then on to Oxford where he majored in the classics, and then to Cambridge. He meant in Massachusetts, not England, but he wanted me to ask about it. When I didn't, he told me Massachusetts.

"I got married shortly after Law School, to the Dean's daughter. He was also the Managing Partner of a distinguished Boston Law Firm. I somehow ended up there. My wife is the President of Far East Families, a 501c(3) nonprofit. They rescue orphan kids from abusive environments over there. We've placed over 125 kids, mostly girls here in the US in the past eight years."

"I love doing this work on adoption more than the actual practice of the law, so I went over to it full time a couple of years ago. In fact, five years ago my wife and I adopted two of the girls who were sisters. We moved to San Francisco to continue to work on adoption matters, and have never looked back."

"I do mostly Pro Bono legal work, all by referral. Having family financial backing is a blessing that lets me do what my heart urges me to do rather than always looking to my clients for money. That's how I ran into Rodney Silvertongue. He and his wife were trying to adopt and were running into a lot of government red tape. We met and he told me the story, and then told me about the winery and how the Bankruptcy people were trying to steal it from him. I told him I would try and help him. I already had a couple of other clients who were experiencing the same frustration with the bankruptcy system as Rodney had experienced, so I had a little background in these bankruptcy controversies."

"What has been your experience with the US Trustee's office, Mr. Freeman?"

"Call me Dex, please. I can't really give you any factual evidence now, but I don't like what I have experienced so far from the US Trustee, Tony Santos. I told him I didn't like the way his staff was treating my client. I thought he was having a bad day when he made threatening remarks toward my client, but I came to realize that his reaction was a major part of his personality. He ordered me to stay out of it. He told me if I stayed involved, I might get more than I bargained for. Let's just say I think that whatever is going on over there, he is a major contributor to the office's reputation of refusing to help people who desperately need help."

I decided this was a man of integrity, and that the employees in the UST office who had spoken despairingly about the man must have had their views poisoned by their boss, US Trustee Tony Santos.

Dexter Freeman continued unloading on me. "You should know, Jeffrey, that I'm conducting my own investigation into Leon Quirk's murder. I've found some pretty interesting information which I'd be willing to share with you if you will tell me some things that you probably know."

All of a sudden, my new friend was trying to cross a line that I could not allow him to cross.

"Dex, as much as I might like to do that, I can't as a government employee. The information I have is all confidential and privileged and for me to do so would be wrong, even if it would eventually help me in the case."

"As a lawyer, I can understand and respect that."

We were done for the night. We split the check and left.

My first cup of coffee the next morning arrived in a paper cup, at 8:45 in Judith Quarles reception room, waiting for her to get off the phone. Zack Callahan had already instructed me to conduct a complete examination of Judith Quarles Trustee bank account, and he had already instructed her to keep her records under lock and key until I arrived. I was to determine if there were similar Swiss deposits and Cayman Island withdrawals like I had found in the Quirk and Amarillo cases.

"I think that Judge Witherspoon, if he's mixed up in this, had a reason to appoint Quarles, and we want to squeeze it out of her." Zack Callahan had suggested to me. "Do you think you're up to this?" Callahan had asked me in his most condescending tone. "You know I am!" I had responded.

"Ms. Quarles is ready to see you now." I was informed through an intercom. I went right in.

I began my entrance conference with Judith Quarles and found she had been a trustee for three years and had been appointed by Judge Anderson, the Chief Bankruptcy judge, not Judge Witherspoon. She was a strikingly beautiful young lady, slender build with reddish curly hair. There was a photo on her desk of her, and presumably of her husband and young daughter. As we chatted, it became apparent to me she was worried about something. I am used to this reaction when I meet people at first, mostly because they are nervous about their financial records. That is a normal reaction. Inspectors of financial records are about as welcome as the flu.

I went to work and thoroughly examined her bank accounts and the case files she had been assigned. I found nothing out of place or even suspicious.

After about a week of examining her records and finding them to have been efficiently maintained, I was wrapping up and getting ready to leave. When I got to the door, she asked me if I would stay; that she had something she needed to talk to me about.

"It's important and I've been afraid to mention it to anyone up until now, but you've been kind and professional and I am going to trust you."

"My friend, Eddie Cruise, is an FBI agent and I think he may need to be a party to this. With your 'ok' I'm going to call him and ask him to come over here." She agreed. Eddie was here in thirty minutes.

Judith began to cry. "This is so embarrassing. This is going to look so bad for me. I know you are investigating Leon Quirk's Bankruptcy cases and his death. Leon was my law professor, in Bankruptcy, Administrative and Commercial law classes. I was failing Commercial law because I just couldn't understand the Uniform Commercial Code, and I went to him, asking for some extra help. He seemed to take an interest in me, and it wasn't long before we were engaged in an affair. He was older that I was, but I liked him and he was very nice to me. After graduation, I broke it off and we went our separate ways."

"Two years later I married and two years after that we had our daughter. The following year my husband went to Afghanistan with the JAG corps. He's been gone two years and won't be back for another six months".

"Then one day, Leon Quirk showed up at my office. I let my guard down and agreed to have dinner with him. One thing led to another, and I soon found myself involved in another affair with him."

Ms. Quarles continued on with her story. The day Quirk was killed, and two days before I showed up to begin my audit, Judith was visited by a Chinese man named Lia Baoshan.

"Sit down and turn off your intercom.......No calls."

He got right to the point. He produced several photographs of her and Quirk, each photograph arranged in order to be more compromising than the previous photograph. Judith said she was shocked to the point of hysteria. Baoshan pressed his advantage.

"I will hold these photographs and not reveal them as long as you obey me exactly. Do I make myself clear?"

"I represent certain powerful off-shore investors. In a couple of months, you will begin to receive deposits from a Swiss bank. You are to deposit these in your Trustee bank account and await my instructions. I will tell you when and how to distribute the funds, using the code names, 'Jennifer Brian'. Do not tell anyone of these arrangements or you will pay the price you do not want to pay."

"Those are the names of my daughter and husband!"

After he finally left, Judith was in a state of total bewilderment. She didn't know where or to whom to turn. The first Swiss deposit was due to come in any day now. She appreciated my approach to the examination of her records and decided to tell me everything.

Eddie asked, "Were you the voice on the phone the day after Quirk was killed?"

"Yes. I was hoping it wasn't true so I called, hoping Leon would answer. When he didn't, I hung up."

The FBI knows exactly how to handle these situations.

"Judith, I want you to do exactly what Baoshan told you to do. Every time you receive a Swiss deposit and every time you are asked to make a disbursement of those funds, I want you to do what he told you to do, and to notify me on this pager."

Eddie and I went to the FBI field office where Eddie called in the name of Lia Baoshan to FBI's Identification Division. Then he and I made a listing of all facts we knew so far relating to the suspected Bay area bankruptcy conspiracy cases.

Trustee Leon Quirk had set a new national standard by embezzling bankruptcy funds in excess of $5,000,000. Included in his Trust bank account, although not a part of the embezzlement charges, were highly suspicious unidentified deposits from a Swiss bank account, equal in total amounts to bank withdrawals to an organization named "Outfront, Inc." to a bank located in the Cayman Islands.

Four other embezzlement cases identified in the Bay area. None of the four embezzlements were anywhere close in amount to the Quirk case, and none of the four had any unidentified deposits or withdrawals except as they pertained to the personal accounts of the Trustee.

The murder of former Trustee Leon Quirk and the subsequent discovery of a note in one of Quirk's shirt pockets containing the name of Zhang Zhimin, a known hit man with the Chinese mafia-type gang, Dragon Rules.

The meeting with Judith Quarles where she revealed the blackmail scheme and the arrangement she had made with a Chinaman named Lia Baoshan.

The very slow response of US Trustee Tony Santos, to criticisms regarding his office, basically ignoring complaints of persons going through bankruptcy, based on his reasoning, not the law or facts.

The firing by Santos of his chief investigator Wyatt Truman for giving me information helpful to my investigation of Leon Quirk, and then claiming Truman was being fired for something that happened years before Truman was hired by Santos was very troublesome.

Bankruptcy Judge Sidney Witherspoon had appointed all five of the Trustees who had been charged with embezzlement. In addition, he had appointed Judith Quarles to take over all of Quirk's cases. This move was strange considering Ms. Quarles ran a clean operation; strange that is until Lia Baoshan approached her with his blackmail plan. Could the Chinese blackmailer be connected to Witherspoon?

We both felt there had to be a common thread to these happenings. Eddie and I agreed we should recommend to Washington that we continue our investigations by concentrating on Bankruptcy Judge Sidney Witherspoon.

The net was getting wider.

CHAPTER 12

From My House to Animal House to the Out House

"It's Washington from Washington on line 2 for Jeffrey," Alice blurted over the intercom before I had even reached my cubbyhole with my morning coffee. She loved to say it that way and told everyone within earshot that "she had invented that way of introducing him and that 'he loved it.'"

Two years earlier after Cyrus Washington had been nominated and then approved as Attorney General, he and his wife had toured the major offices of the Department of Justice. San Francisco was an important stop along the way, and his tour included a meeting with US Trustee Santos.

"Yessir. I can put you through now. I hope you have a nice day, also, Sir. And say 'hello' to Clarice for me, please. Let her know that my Asters and Zinnias are really blooming this summer. Thank you. Here's Jeffrey, I mean, Mr. Allan." Alice also liked to remind the office that she was "a good friend" with the wife of the Attorney General, and that they had discussed gardening when the Washingtons had visited. Their visit had pre-dated my arrival here and her meeting with Ms. Washington seemed to make Alice feel good about herself, and I was certainly in favor of that.

Getting a call from the AG first thing in the morning was a Big Deal. He had hundreds of attorneys working for him, and it was a big ego booster to me that he had taken a special interest in "my" case. There were many US Attorneys who never got such a phone call from him, and here was I, a "bean counter" I think I was called by the local Assistant US Attorney, receiving special attention from one of the most influential leaders of the United States Government. Jeffrey Allan, you certainly have arrived. Now, if I just don't screw this thing up.

The purpose of his call was to caution me that he did not want any action I might take to tip off Judge Witherspoon that he might be a "person of interest" in this case.

"I don't want to alert anyone we suspect anything. Just let them keep doing what they've been doing. Put a watch on Ms. Quarles so she's safe. Should we be protecting anyone else? What about that lawyer? What's his name again? Friedman, Freeman, whatever? You know who I mean. Could he be a target? What's your gut telling you, Jeffrey?"

I was tempted to answer, "I don't know, Sir," but I did know. I admit, I was a bit intimidated about being asked my opinion by the Attorney General of the United States, but these people were in danger, and I knew in my heart that I must not be afraid to say it. I had met and had interaction with both people, Quarles and Freeman, and I liked them and believed they added value to our cases. I was not going to remain silent, knowing them to be in harm's way. This was the first time I'd been asked to make a judgment call on a matter that had life and death consequences, and I was going to give it.

"If this group could kill Quirk, they wouldn't hesitate to eliminate Judith Quarles and Dexter Freeman." I didn't include myself on that list, but I am there. "Remember, they've got that Chinese hit man on their payroll. If he was able to get to Quarles or Freeman, that guy could kill them and disappear into Canada or abroad."

"I'll set up protection details for both of them. Let me remind you, Jeffrey, that our neighbors to the north have a much more open borders approach to immigration than we do. I had better alert our guys on the border, just in case."

"Yes, Sir. Good idea."

I ended my side of the conversation by recommending I search for the connection between Witherspoon and Santos. This was immediately approved.

I thought about this all the way home to our motel room that evening. I found Rebecca standing near the door with an "I need to talk to you" look on her face. Even I could tell that she wanted my undivided attention.

"Cordie, we need to talk." She always saved the use of my middle name for important news. Her look and tone gave me "goose bumps." I had already decided that my office work was now in second place to her agenda.

"We're going to have a baby! You're going to be a daddy."

My world absolutely stopped.

I was a hair away from passing out. No, I'd better not do that. I've got to sit down. No, that's not right. I've got to hug her. That's the right move. Good boy, Jeffrey. You've got it right! I can pass out later; I can sit down tonight. I've got to hug this girl now.

It occurred to me that Becca had been so wonderful and patient and understanding to me all during this case I was involved in. At times I caught myself just going through the motions as far as our conversations were concerned. It's like this case had taken over my entire life.

I had often day dreamed of what it would be like to be a father one day. If it was a boy, I would want him to play little league baseball just like I had wanted to do, and if a girl she would be all soft and cuddly and spotless and sweet just like Becca.

Suddenly I felt like I had a special purpose in life, and it wasn't just about catching bad guys. It was more about Rebecca and me being able to help form our part of the next generation. It was an awesome responsibility to be sure, and one I thought we were up to.

Becca and I talked a lot about this during the next few hours. We decided that she could continue to work at the law firm but that she had to do everything her doctor recommended her to do, like rest and diet.

It was an awesome feeling to know I was going to be able to personally influence a member of the next generation! That was a big thrill, but also a huge responsibility. I was determined to become committed to balancing my work with what would be expected of me as a father and husband. I thought I was finally beginning to mature spiritually as a man.

Back at work I plunged into my research of the backgrounds of Judge Witherspoon and Tony Santos. I decided to begin with the FBI file, thanks to Eddie, on Judge Witherspoon.

Judge Sidney Witherspoon was one of seven bankruptcy judges who serviced the Northern District of California. He had been on the bench for five years, having previously served two years in the US Trustee's office in Washington, mostly as a young assistant to the head of the office. His record revealed nothing outstanding, good or bad. There was, however, this notation in his Personnel File from his former boss, a man now deceased. "Sid does his work and sticks to himself, but seems to want to take credit for anything good that happens that he's involved in, and is quick to deny that any negative results are his fault."

Interesting reading, huh? Kind of amateur psychology stuff. I made a note of it and brought it up to Rebecca later that night. I never discussed specific case related items with her, but just mentioned it in a general sense as being a "comment found in a file" about a guy we might be going to question.

Ever the practical, honest witness, she asked: "Would you even pay attention to a comment like that if you read it about yourself in a file? Couldn't that be said about a lot of ambitious young people?"

Her advice was: "Don't completely ignore it. Just be careful of being an amateur psychologist. You don't have that man's boss around to ask if he could expand on his notation. Can you ask Eddie if he can get you that other guy's file and compare the two?"

Yikes! Who was the investigator in our family, anyhow? I quietly thanked God for her.

The next day I was back in the hunt.

"Hey, Eddie, do you have anything in your file on Santos I might be able to use?"

Pay Dirt.

Comparing the early life of Santos and Witherspoon, I found that although they had attended different law schools, they both had attended the University of California Berkeley together through their junior year. Both had transferred to a different college for their senior year. I went to the California Berkeley campus library and there I was able to determine that both Witherspoon and Santos had belonged to the same fraternity. It was located on Arch Street, just off the campus, located in what used to be a family dwelling. Walking up the walkway to the house, thoughts of my unborn son or daughter came to me and I thought my own child might one day choose this path for his early life and only one conclusion suggested itself: "Party Animal!" Holy smoke. My unborn child was already affecting my life!

I thought this to be a typical fraternity house, slightly shabby and rundown, with paint peelings, brown patch splotchy grass and parts of a fallen gutter lying in what used to be a garden. The neighborhood was full of such relics of a bygone era of unearned affluence and indulgence. Both the outside and inside reminded me of the movie from the seventy's, "Animal House"; empty beer cans thrown near the trash cans, and a half-empty liquor bottle lying open on a table near the doorway. All we needed was the appearance of John Belushi. Apparently, there were no rules regarding drinking. The frat guy serving as "guard duty" showed me around a place that didn't appear clean and smelled bad.

I kept telling myself: "Put your feelings on hold, Jeffrey. You're being judgmental about a life you didn't ever have. You have a job to do."

Off the main hall was the wood-paneled library with the fake fireplace and shelves filed with memorabilia.

"Can you show me how to find some pictures of guys who lived here in particular years?" I asked the guy showing me around. I tried hard not to sound like a cop in a fraternity house.

I found the pictures of both Witherspoon and Santos. Then I found something I hadn't bargained on. A group photograph with Witherspoon and Santos along with Leon Quirk and Amarillo Trustee Adolph Riddler!

I went immediately to the college library and looked in that year's yearbook and found all four of them. I made copies of the relevant photos. Then almost by accident I noticed that the yearbook had been dedicated to a very pretty young Oriental woman who had died during the year of unexplained causes.

The name of the woman, Long, was a typical Chinese sounding name. Since there was so little information I went to the *San Francisco Chronicle*'s office, and in her obituary, there was a listing of her family members. I made copies of the obit and headed back to Eddie's office, thinking I might have found a link.

Eddie checked the names of the dead girl's family members and got an immediate response. Included in the girl's relatives was the name, Long Ziqlang, her grandfather. Further FBI information revealed him to be the Godfather of a Chinese organized crime family known as Dragon Rules. In San Francisco, these guys were well-known to have a mafia-like structure similar to the crime families of the East and Midwest areas of the United States. They were reputed to be every bit as ruthless and powerful. However, none had ever been convicted in a court of law.

I remembered this was the same gang that Zhang Zhimin, the mysterious name on the crumpled piece of paper located in the shirt pocket of slain embezzler Leon Quirk, belonged to. This was either a huge coincidence or another piece of the puzzle. This could eventually tie the bankruptcy corruption cases together.

Eddie got the FBI file on the grandfather, Long Ziqlang, which we reviewed together. Two or more agents reviewing the same file was a common FBI technique proven to get better results, but new to me.

Long Ziqlang had been deported from China because of his connections to organized crime. He got a special visa to live in the United States. That didn't make any sense to me. None the less it happened. It was during one of these years in the United States that his granddaughter had died of an undisclosed illness. When Long Ziqlang's visa expired, he was nowhere to be found. He was able to stay one step ahead of law enforcement because he made sure others within his organization were loyal and were able to help him stay one step ahead of the immigration authorities.

Eddie summed it up: "He spread money around and had a friend on the inside at immigration."

"Can you check those other fraternity member names out on your data base, Eddie?"

Several came back, mostly referring to sensitive job application clearances. One in particular was of interest to us. Joshua Peterson, now a San Mateo policeman.

We headed just south of San Francisco to the working class section of San Mateo to see if Peterson could give us any information.

"While you were up at Berkeley, Dexter Freeman called. Seems he just located some documents he said would be of interest to us in our case, but didn't want to discuss it on the phone."

"He did insist that what he had found would prove there was corruption in the entire bankruptcy system in the Bay area. He promised to lay it all out for us if we could arrange to meet him. It may be another dead end, but I thought we had better see what he has. I called Larry Albright and got approval to set up a meeting for tonight. I have already made reservations for us for a motel room in Santa Rosa. I need you there with me."

I called Rebecca to let her know I wouldn't be home until late that night.

When we got to Peterson's house, we caught him mowing his lawn. That's why he hadn't answered the phone when Eddie tried to call him before we left the office.

Peterson said he would be delighted to talk to us.

"Can you tell us anything about your fraternity association with either Leon Quirk or Adolph Riddler?" Eddie didn't mention any other name because we didn't want to take a chance that Peterson might be involved too. We didn't want it to get back to Santos or Witherspoon that they might be persons of interest in our case.

Peterson launched into some funny stories about frat stunts the whole fraternity had been involved in, and then he told us that several of his frat brothers had become friends with some students from China and had ended their time at Berkeley by spending more time with the exchange students than they spent with their fraternity brothers. Quirk and Riddler were among that group.

"Never saw one without the other," he volunteered.

Both of them left Berkeley at the end of their Junior year and went to different schools, he had heard, for their senior year. Peterson was asked if he could remember any of the names of other members of that group, but Peterson said he couldn't remember, but would call us if he did remember.

"Funny thing is I think they all became lawyers and worked for the government. Had something to do with Bankruptcy, I think...."

That evening, Larry Albright, Eddie, and I arrived early at the Santa Rosa motel and awaited Dexter Freeman's arrival.

Ten o'clock came and went. No Dexter Freeman. We waited until 11:30 and finally gave it up. Eddie tried the cell phone number he had been given, but there was no answer there either. Discouraged, we all went home.

The next morning Eddie tried again but still no answer. He called Freeman's office and spoke with the receptionist.

"I don't have any idea where he is and that's very unlike him. People who have appointments are waiting for him. I'll call you when I know something."

She wasn't just giving us the old secretarial cover. We went from "upset with him" to "concerned about him" real fast.

There was no contact with him at all that day, and the receptionist sounded worried when Eddie talked to her again just before five. He had never just disappeared before. My only previous personal contact with Freeman was our dinner at the Italian restaurant. I hadn't gotten the impression he was irresponsible.

His behavior was out of character.

CHAPTER 13

Texas Two-Step

It's next to impossible to keep a shocking story out of the grist mill of the twenty- four hour Cable News cycle today. If it involves a famous or infamous person, not a chance. Dexter Freeman had already made himself known to news outlets, so his disappearance would certainly qualify as newsworthy. Some insider would certainly spill it to the press.

The following morning Dexter's wife phoned the sheriff personally to report Dexter's disappearance. She pleaded with him to keep his disappearance confidential, and because she and Dexter had helped finance his last campaign, she thought she had a shot of keeping it quiet. It only took about an hour for it to make the rounds. By the time I got to my office space, it was the buzz of the US Trustee office. Since most of the staff thought Freeman to be a loose cannon anyway, the remarks were mostly derogatory.

"He must have complained to the wrong people."

"I'll bet he's stashed away with a woman somewhere."

"Well, maybe we've seen the last of him up here."

"I'll bet Santos isn't shedding a tear."

The following day, the *San Francisco Chronicle* began a series of stories, quoting "reliable sources" about corruption and secret deals within the bankruptcy system involving "millions of dollars of unaccounted for bankruptcy funds." There was a lot of speculation, as there always is when something happens to a person who has been in the news…..The price we pay for our First Amendment rights.

By the time the Evening News was broadcast, Ms. Freeman was center stage on three networks, broadcasting from her driveway.

"Ms. Freeman, do you have any idea where your husband is?"

"Has he ever done this before?"

"Is there any money missing from your bank accounts?" "Have you checked them?" "When was the last time?"

"Have you suspected your husband was having an affair with someone?"

On and on it went. Finally, exasperated, she faced the vultures and said, "Go find yourselves another victim to harass." With that, she turned around, went inside her house, and slammed the door shut behind her.

Two days past, and still no reliable word about the missing lawyer. The usual "off the wall" calls came into the FBI from South Dakota, Michigan, and the Ozarks, claiming to have seen Dexter riding on a motorcycle with a young blond woman behind him, or other such nonsense.

Finally, a body was discovered below a steep drop off near a parking area just past the Golden Gate Bridge. The man had been shot twice in the back of the head with a small caliber weapon, probably the preferred .22 cal, the gangland pass to eternity. Soon afterwards, dental records confirmed the body to be that of Dexter Freeman.

The news media went ballistic with speculation about Freeman being ambushed while on his way to a meeting with Justice Department officials. The US Attorney's office was swamped with calls from all over the nation on the murder.

Local Law Enforcement grew impatient with the horde of reporters harassing them with inquiries, so they issued the statement they always do in order to get the pressure off them.

"There is no evidence that Mr. Freeman had been targeted by anyone, and our investigation has concluded that the victim may have stopped in the parking area to relieve himself and was apparently shot by someone hiding in wait for anyone to stop. We believe Mr. Freeman was a victim who happened to be in the wrong place at the wrong time."

End of investigation.

Eddie immediately labeled that conclusion as "bullshit." So did I. So did the ballistics report from the FBI crime lab. They were the best in the world. The hit was identical to the hit on Leon Quirk. Same type ammo, .22 cal, Hi Speed LR, Same gun. Browning Buckmark. Someone had gotten word of the meeting Freeman and Eddie had set up and made sure he was eliminated before he could talk. Eddie and I both got instructions from the AG as to what our next course of action should be.

Eddie and I were to "scrub the documents" I had received from Adolph Riddler's Amarillo bank, meaning we should review all of them looking for anything that might have been overlooked. Up to now, I had only given my attention to the bank deposits from the Swiss bank and the disbursements to the account in the Cayman Island. But there were hundreds of other documents that could produce a lead to follow.

When I was in Amarillo the first time, I had made a listing of all cases assigned to Riddler, and then when Joseph LaSalle and I went to Lubbock, I reviewed the Amarillo case files stored there, and had made photocopies of all relevant documents. This was to be our starting point. We next had to understand how Riddler catalogued his documents. Each Regional Bankruptcy Trustee in the Federal Bankruptcy System had their own system of cataloguing documents. We had to familiarize ourselves with the system in use in West Texas. Their system was different than the systems Eddie and I were used to. This was mostly boring and tedious work.

We were looking for a pattern of behavior. We sorted every piece of paper three ways: by maker/author, and then a separate listing by payee/recipient and finally by subject. We did the same with copies of checks and deposits. That meant three photocopies of each document. This was before computer systems that could do in seconds what it took us hours to unravel.

This process revealed something vitally important to the outcome we were looking for. When Riddler would close a case, he would get an order from the bankruptcy judge for his compensation. Rather than write the checks to himself, he made the checks payable to the same Cayman Islands bank account that the payments to the mysterious company, "Outfront, Inc." were going to. It wasn't illegal, but we sure wanted to know "why."

Back in my makeshift cubbyhole in the UST office was a note to call Callahan.

"Jeffrey, the AG wants to talk to you about your report, and I think he wants you to go back to Amarillo and interview Adolph Riddler. He said he would call you. He believes there's a better chance Riddler will talk to you alone than if he was to send an FBI agent to interview him, and I think he's right. However, if you go, I want you to take someone with you."

This brought to mind my first trip to West Texas which ended with my fellow crime-fighter, Joseph LaSalle, being murdered while sitting in the car next to me. That image will haunt me forever.

Once again my thoughts turned to our unborn baby and its future with and without a daddy. I decided to call Rebecca and tell her of with my fears.

"Cordie, you haven't been trained for this kind of stuff. That's Eddie's job."

"I know, but I don't want to give the impression that I'm not up for this assignment."

"Why don't you tell them that you will go, but you have to have someone with you who can protect you? It would help a lot if you would ask God to protect you while you're there."

"You may have to help me out on that. The only prayer I can remember is one I recited as a child. I think it started out, 'Now I lay me down to sleep.' I can't remember the rest of it."

And she prayed for me right there. I instantly felt more relaxed with the change of focus. I thanked her for the help and prayer, and she thanked me for the call.

I was blessed.

All of a sudden, the intercom blurted out Alice's newfound ego booster.

"It's Washington from Washington on line 4 for Jeffrey."

The AG began by outlining his expectations for me to accomplish with Riddler. I snuck in something new in the middle of his instructions. "Sir, you know how you're always mentioning working in teams rather than alone? So, I wanted to ask you if you thought it would be a good idea for me to take someone from the FBI along, given what happened last time I was there?"

"Yeah, that might be a good idea now that you bring it up. You bankruptcy guys haven't been trained to carry and use a weapon, so why don't you get one of those guys from the San Fran office to go with you. I caution you, though, don't let whoever you take tip off Riddler that he's FBI. Know what I mean?"

One quick phone call and Eddie had freed up his schedule to go.

Once there, I talked Eddie into visiting the famous Big Texas Steak Ranch before confronting Riddler. This time I ordered the Porterhouse, but just the eighteen ounce one rather than the seventy-two ounce. I had to work all afternoon and I didn't want to get sleepy!

Riddler's eyes narrowed when I walked into his office. I didn't know if it was because he just didn't like me, or because of the "bodyguard" I had with me, whom I introduced as my assistant, Eddie. I explained he was along to take notes because I had hurt my hand and couldn't write. I could have saved my breath. Riddler was still as belligerent as he was the first time I met him.

"I'm not going to let you see my financial records. They're confidential."

"Sorry, you don't have that option. I already have all of your deposit information and copies of your checks. So if you want to avoid a Contempt of Court citation, Mr. Riddler, you'll give me everything we need to complete our investigation."

He was clearly not used to being cut off at the waist, but Eddie and I had already agreed on the strategy.

"All I need from you, Mr. Riddler, is an explanation of the deposits you made from a Swiss bank that had no apparent connection with any bankruptcy cases you were assigned, and an explanation of the payment of those funds to an account in the Cayman Islands."

It was a beautiful sight to see the look on Riddler's face. It was as white as the sheet of paper Eddie was writing on.

"I've done nothing wrong. I followed the rules for everything, every procedure, every regulation. I run a first-class operation here. There might be some things I can't explain off the top of my head, but my accountant can when he gets here in a couple of days. Why don't you have your assistant here make a list of the entries you're interested in and we'll give you an explanation on every one."

I began by reciting the details of each Swiss deposit, and the corresponding checks disbursing the funds. After about thirty minutes of constant pressure, there was a noticeable change in his attitude. He told me he needed to talk to his attorney before he would talk any further with me.

Riddler met us the next morning at his office without his attorney.

"I'm afraid to talk to anyone about those deposits or checks. You don't know these people. They're dangerous."

"Well, who are they? How do you know them? What are you afraid of? We can get you protection." I wanted to tell him that protection was sitting right next to me, but I didn't. Wisdom overruled emotion.

Riddler began to give us the real story, and Eddie started taking notes. I loved it!

"I went to Berkeley and there were four of us that became really close. We did everything together, majored in business, but mostly partying. We became friendly with a group of Chinese foreign exchange students. The University and our fraternity made a deal with us to absorb part of our college tuition and fraternity dues in exchange for mentoring these students into the college social life. There were ten or twelve of them and they didn't seem like bad people, just lost in America. It was easy money and it didn't hurt anybody."

"So, what was the problem? Did they want you to smuggle in anything, like drugs or people?"

"Not at first. They were pretty secretive, stuck to themselves, even at the fraternity. I met the sister of one of them and really fell for her. She was beautiful and smart. We became involved. She invited me to her family's restaurant for dinner and I got to meet the rest of her family. They were very kind and good to me."

"One Sunday night I told her I couldn't keep our date because I had a migraine and I was afraid to drive with one. She told me she had a wonderful drug that cured migraines. She said the drug came from the mountains of Thailand. An hour later she and her grandfather picked me up and gave me the drug to take. He said to me, 'You don't have AB Negative blood, do you?' He explained AB Negative was the only blood type the drug resisted. He claimed the drug cured back and body pain, hangovers, headaches, even toothaches. Mei Hua said the drug was being marketed by her grandfather's company first, and then all over the world. She said there were no negative effects as long as the consumer didn't have AB Negative blood."

"Mei Hua confided in me later that she had blood type AB Negative, and had been warned by her grandfather to never take the drug."

"But she took it anyway, and I didn't do anything to discourage her. One evening she and I took the drug and we were so relaxed we went to sleep. When I awoke she was still sleeping. I tried to awaken her but I got no response."

"She never awoke from her sleep. Her name meant 'Beautiful Flower' in Mandarin. She certainly was that. If you had known her you would know how perfect that name was for her."

"When an autopsy was performed at her grandfather's insistence, the Coroner found no trace of any known drug and called her death: 'Natural Causes'. Her grandfather had the perfect cover for his drug."

He claimed he never heard from the grandfather directly again.

After law school, Riddler got his Trusteeship through the influence of his fraternity brother, Tony Santos, who by then had a top job in the US Trustee's office.

One day about four years ago, an Oriental man showed up at his office, unannounced, and identified himself as a business partner of Mei Hua's grandfather. The old man needed a favor and wondered if Riddler could help. The man identified himself as a lawyer in China.

"My client, Mr. Ziqlang, owns a business that has developed an electronic devise which certain foreign investors are trying to steal." He went on to explain Riddler would be getting funds from a Swiss bank, and Riddler would receive instructions on how to disburse the funds. The oriental man insisted there was nothing illegal about the operation. He also told Riddler he would be compensated well.

Riddler claimed he told the man that he was not interested, but the man was insistent that Riddler's refusal was not the act of a friend. He said he would return and hoped Riddler would change his mind.

A week later Riddler found his pet German shepherd dead on his front porch. Later that evening the oriental man again appeared, this time at Riddler's home. This time the strange man went directly to the reason for the visit. He wanted Riddler to know that his client knew about him and his client's dead granddaughter both taking the drug the old man had warned her against, and that the grandfather held Riddler responsible for his granddaughter's death. Riddler needed to reconsider his earlier refusal because his client could be a very persuasive man, and that an act of refusal could be very unhealthy for Riddler.

The man went on to explain that the dead girl's parents needed financial help and that Riddler was in a position to help in the amount of $500.00 per week for the rest of their lives. For this "help," the grandfather would be able to guarantee Riddler protection against any government agency that questioned the transactions. The man emphasized to Riddler that he wasn't asking this time; he was setting the rules for Riddler to live a long and healthy life.

Riddler rationalized with himself that there would be no falsification of any records, nothing that could be traced back to him, no smuggling, no drug money. In short, he believed there were very slim chances that these foreign transactions would be connected to him. More to the point, he was afraid to say "No."

I showed him in the Trustee handbook that the trust account was never to be used for anything except Trustee business.

"Mr. Riddler, it is apparent you are in clear violation of the agreement you signed with the Office of the US Trustee. You are in breach of your contract and under the terms of that contract, you can be removed from your Trustee responsibilities immediately. I want to talk with my boss at our office in Washington and let them decide what to do about your conduct."

I didn't want to put all our cards on the table just then. I was feeling pretty heady about the results of our interview so far, but I wanted to see how we could work this leverage to get more information and perhaps a lead to solving the entire case. I was on a role. I instructed Riddler: "to continue to receive and distribute the maverick funds just as you have been doing. You must follow the disbursement instructions exactly as the man gives them to you. Notify me by beeper each time there is a transaction involving these funds. Lastly, you absolutely must not disclose to anyone the details of our visit here today. Do you understand?"

"Yes, sir."

"As part of our agreement, I will not notify the local authorities about the threats against you until we are able to get a handle on the people, activities, and program of the grandfather's company."

While I believed some of what Riddler told me I had a strong feeling that he didn't tell me everything. If Riddler was really an innocent participant he could have called the Office of the US Trustee and received protection from the US Marshalls. Riddler's lack of memory on the identity of the grandfather, or the identity of his Chinese visitor was also troublesome. I had been careful not to reveal to Riddler that the grandfather had already been identified as Dragon Rules leader, Long Ziqlang. I was also reasonably sure that my visit had already been reported to the real kingpins of the illegal operations.

This knowledge struck fear in my heart. I could end up like Dexter Freeman.

Would I live to be a father to our unborn child?

On the way back to San Francisco, Eddie and I went over the notes he had taken. I complimented him on his demeanor and reasonably good secretarial skills. "If you ever want to leave the FBI, I'd give you a good recommendation." I know there will be a day of reckoning from "Fast Eddie." He was too good a friend not to retaliate in kind.

These thoughts and more consumed my time until we landed in San Francisco.

CHAPTER 14

The Pandora Box

"Whaddya mean, this place isn't safe!" I really didn't expect Rebecca to answer my question because we had been over this before. I learned from Eddie that the first two rules about pregnant wives were that they could request any food at any time, day or night, and that they could make statements completely without notice or contest. This was of the second variety. Eddie had too many easy answers for me. "She's just responding to her God-given nesting instinct, Buddy. Better start helping her find a better place."

Ever since our break in a few weeks ago, Rebecca had been on the hunt for another place to live. She found several possibilities, but they were all out of our price range. I got in on the hunt right away, but it became almost a full-time job and one of those was enough. I couldn't seem to split my brain to do two things at the same time. Rebecca had a constant struggle with morning sickness and other issues. She had to spend almost an entire month in bed....doctor's orders. I didn't have the energy to challenge that as I was too busy finding her a pizza at 3 a.m. or a Banana Split before breakfast.

The rents for apartments in San Francisco seemed outrageous to one from the mountains of North Georgia, but the possibilities were plentiful. Although we both were on a housing allowance from our employers, our combined allowance was still below what the market demanded. I expressed my frustration to Callahan, and he agreed to bump my allowance up to the point where we might be able to afford lower middle-class accommodations.

We found a nice, bright, two-bedroom with a den/office, nice kitchen, living room with a gas fireplace, located on the fifth floor of a high-rise apartment, and still within walking distance to downtown. Better than average security, and the guys from Eddie's office retrofitted it like Ft. Knox. I was a hero again at home. That was my real objective in this mission.

I arrived at our new residence late at night after dropping Eddie off at his home, and climbed into bed besides Rebecca. Just as I did, the luminous dial noted that it was ten minutes past one, just enough time for me to get almost six hours of rest for my still travelling brain.

Eddie on the phone for me first thing in the morning was often too much for me. In the old days, I would have let Rebecca get it, but my new pre-daddy self grabbed it to save her.

"6:30 isn't too early for you, is it Jeff?" Without waiting for an answer, he added: "Meet me at the Donut place around the corner from you in half an hour. We might finally have a big break in our case. Tell you about it then." And then he was gone. Conversation is overrated anyhow, right?

Despite not being a morning person and the fact that eight hours ago I was still on the plane, I made it there in twenty-five minutes. Eddie was already on his second cup of coffee.

"What's so important that it couldn't wait until we got to the office? I left so early I didn't even have a chance to shave."

Eddie had a gleam in his eyes that hadn't been there for a while. "It looks like we've gotten a big break, Buddy. Just listen to me for a few minutes, ok?"

"Last night Freeman's wife, Donna, called. Rummaging through some of Dexter's things she found the key to a safe deposit box in a Wells Fargo envelope. There was a copy of a signature card with only Dexter's name on it. She hadn't remembered any time they had banked at Wells Fargo, and she wants to check it out. She already called the bank and the branch manager is going to let her have access to it, even though her signature is not on file with them. Seems they have been keeping up with her husband's disappearance by watching the local news, and they are trying to help, or so she thinks. Anyway, she wants me to go with her, and I want you to come along as a witness to whatever we find in the box. She wants me to meet her in the bank lobby at 9 a.m."

Eddie continued. "I know, I know. It may mean nothing, and we take the chance that the contents may be something completely unrelated to our case, but I think it's worth taking a look. Suppose the contents reveal something about her husband that would destroy his good name? Cast suspicions on him? What if there is something that shows he had another woman stashed away somewhere? She's a brave lady who believes in her husband. She's willing to risk her beliefs to see if there's something in that box that might give a clue to who murdered her husband. "

I spoke up. "I'm betting that she knew her husband pretty well."

We were headed into uncharted waters. The lock box contained three photos taken, perhaps by Freeman, along with a sealed envelope. There was nothing else in the box.

The first photo showed three men together: US Trustee Tony Santos, Judge Sidney Witherspoon, and an elderly Oriental man we suspected would be either mafia-head Long Ziqlang or one of his henchmen. No wonder the photo was kept in a secret place! One other photo was of a Dauphin Hi-speed eight-seat helicopter, and third there was a picture of a bridge that we couldn't quite place.

We then opened the sealed envelope. There was a single sheet of paper with only a longhand written notation: BB-veep-6/15.

That was it. No explanation of what the notation meant.

Eddie and I sat in his car for a long time mulling over what had been uncovered. We were puzzled to the point of silence. Finally, Eddie spoke up.

"Well, the good thing was, there wasn't anything in that box to disparage the name of Dexter Freeman."

"What do we do with the photo of Santos, Witherspoon, and whoever that third man is standing with them?"

"I'm going to send it to FBI headquarters to see if our crime lab can help, or if someone in the ID section can identify the Chinaman. I would say that Santos and Witherspoon have a lot to answer to right now without us finding anything else.

"What about the notation in the envelope? That's strange. I can't imagine what that means."

"I'm going to send that on too. Copy that notation in your notebook. You might find something later that sheds light on it."

I asked Donna Freeman if that was her husband's writing on the note. She confirmed it was and said the sheet of paper looked like it was from a notepad on his desk at home. This may have been what Freeman was going to explain to us the night he was murdered.

We did not know who was trustworthy. Certainly not anyone at the US Trustee's office. Eddie felt pretty safe about his office but didn't feel free to discuss the case with anyone other than the SAC.

We knew that even with the photos, if Santos or Witherspoon were confronted, they could say they were "just having a chat with an old friend we had gone to college with." If this case was ever going to get solved, we both knew we had to have some proof that would stick. What we had now was nothing more than suspicion and speculation.

Both of us reported our findings to our respective offices in Washington. The AG left me a message telling me to "talk to Donna Freeman again." Eddie's boss told him the same thing. Eddie had done a little of this already when she had called about the existence of the bank lockbox.

She was surprised to see us when she opened the door.

"Back again so soon? Can't seem to get rid of you guys."

Eddie ignored her bad attempt at humor. "Do you remember Dexter discussing any of his bankruptcy clients with you?"

"No, not really. That was sort of 'out of bounds' for us, even though I did a lot of secretarial work for him when he worked out of home. He claimed there was too much incriminating or embarrassing stuff in those cases and he tried to keep me insulated from the most unpleasant side of his practice."

Eddie and I looked at each other. Eddie turned toward me and rolled his eyes, telling me that he didn't buy what she was selling. He aimed his next shot right at the target.

"If you didn't know any of these people why did you say you suspected something when you found the safe deposit box key?"

She didn't have an answer for that. Finally, she began to open up.

"I got a phone call the night the police found Dexter. The caller wouldn't identify himself. He claimed he was only trying to help me, but I must keep quiet about anything Dexter might have told me about any cases he was working on. He said that if I knew anything it would be best for me to forget about what I knew, and that if I told anyone about this phone call, I would regret it. He ended the call by telling me he would stay in contact with me, and that I had nothing to fear unless I talked to the authorities or betrayed his instructions."

"That's the only contact I've had with him. He hasn't called back."

At that moment, the phone rang. Neither Eddie nor I paid any attention as we both thought it was probably someone paying their condolences to the widow. However, Donna turned pale as she listened to what the caller told her.

"Oh! My! God! We're being watched! You shouldn't be here! Now, my children's lives are in danger! He just told me said he knew that you two were in here with me and that I had to keep quiet and get rid of you now or we were about to have a very bad accident!"

We were clearly being observed by someone who had probably been posted as a lookout ever since Freeman's murder.

We both looked outside, but could see nothing suspicious. There was no doubt, though, that someone knew we were here talking to Donna Freeman. Eddie called the US Marshall's office and about forty-five minutes later, two plain clothed Deputy Marshalls showed up. We stationed one inside the front door and one at the back.

Eddie kept probing with the nervous widow about whether she had any other information she could share with us.

"I can't tell you anything more, and I'm begging you to please leave now."

Whether or not she had something else, we weren't going to get it this day. We both agreed she was a very brave, but a scared and shaken lady.

We each notified Washington and the responses were immediate. "Get to Witherspoon fast. We've got to know what he knows. He's got the weakest character of all the suspects. Every minute you put it off, you run the risk of him getting 'whacked'.

Get to it NOW." AG Cyrus Washington had a lot of experience with these Mafioso types and was familiar with their vernacular.

I was assigned to go with Eddie because of my expertise in bankruptcy matters. Eddie's knowledge of bankruptcy law was confined to his studies while at Georgetown, but he had been trained in interviewing techniques. Eddie's job was to interview the judge. My job was to be present, remain quiet, and take notes.

The judge started off somewhat aggressively.

"I don't know why you gentlemen are here or what information you may think I have that can help you, but let me remind you that I am a Federal judge, appointed by the President of the United States. I have been on the Federal Bench for many years and my reputation is without blemish. I also have a very full calendar with many cases needing adjudication and many people waiting to receive money to be made whole. So, every minute I'm sitting here allowing you to waste my time asking me questions about heaven only knows what, there's someone out there who's been taken advantage of by not getting what they're entitled to."

Eddie was not deterred.

"Thank you for your dedication to your work, Your Honor. We're respectful of your time and we'll be as brief as possible, but may I remind you, for the record, we're investigating evidence of a criminal conspiracy in the Bankruptcy Court that has already resulted in two murders."

"Let me also remind you that my name is Eddie Cruise, and I am a Special Agent with the FBI, and that lying to an FBI agent is punishable by a minimum of five years in a Federal Penitentiary, loss of position in the government, and the forfeiture of a license to practice law, as well as fines. This is 18 US Code, Section 1001. It is a Felony."

"We're not going to put you under oath today, but we don't need to in order that these penalties go into effect. They are in effect now. Do you understand that lying, per se, triggers the Statute and creates the offense?"

Judge Witherspoon sat in his chair with his mouth open, not knowing how to respond.

"Please say 'yes' out loud, sir, so that my secretary, Mr. Allan here, can hear you and make note of it. He is also recoding this session for your protection. Do you understand, sir?"

I thought I noticed a slight flicker of a smirk on Eddie's face. He had "killed two birds with one stone." He had scored a major blow to the judge's assertiveness, and he had paid me back for publicly describing him as my secretary on our recent trip to Amarillo.

The interview began with the judge being reservedly polite, but answering in mostly long, self-serving phrases.

"No, I never showed any favoritism toward former Trustee Leon Quirk or any other Trustee."

"No, Trustee Quirk was never a personal friend of mine."

"Yes, I knew him in college, but we were never close."

"Of course, I was never aware of Quirk's embezzlement schemes."

"Never heard of Quirk being an owner of 'Shebrooke' or any other asset that he had been in charge of as Trustee."

"Don't know anything about any organization called 'Outfront, Inc.'"

"Of course, I don't know who might have killed Quirk. Why would you ask me that? Before his embezzlement schemes, I thought him to be an excellent Trustee. I was sorry to learn of his death."

"No, I do not know any trustee from Amarillo, Texas. Well, wait a minute. Yes, I believe I do remember Adolph Riddler. We weren't close friends, though."

"No, I do not know the name of the elderly Chinese man who was present when I was visiting some close Chinese friends of mine. Seems like I remember some old guy who was always present, but I never knew his name."

Eddie was careful not to mention US Trustee Tony Santo's name here as he did not want Witherspoon to know Santos was a big part of our investigation.

Eddie's continued to question the judge about his college associates. The more Eddie pressed him, the more Witherspoon sweated. Finally, he declined to answer any more questions. The interview was over.

I spent the next day going over the notes I had taken, listening to the tape of the interview, and reviewing the documents I had received from Riddler's trust bank account. I also visited with Trustee Judith Quarles and made copies of all recent deposits she made from the Swiss bank account as well as all recent disbursements made to Outfront, Inc.

This was the ending of a long week for me. I headed home to be with Rebecca.

CHAPTER 15

Vanished!

All the way home, I thought about my assignment here, and how much it had twisted and turned since I first started to look for bankruptcy fraud. Now the Leon Quirk fraud looked trivial compared with what Eddie and I had on our plates. It looked like the San Francisco US Trustee was corrupt; the judge was corrupt; several key players in this mess were dead; millions of dollars had been siphoned away from deserving creditors.

How far did it go?

What would we find next?

Who will be the next victim?

On and on. My mind raced out of control.

The one saving grace in all of this was Rebecca. Our baby would be here in a few months, a responsibility I really was looking forward to, a job I knew I would really like. We were living in a nice condo now, and looking forward to getting back to Helen, Georgia soon. I was so thankful for Rebecca, for the privilege of sharing our lives together. All in all, I was thankful for the blessings I had been showered with. I was beginning to sense something beyond me was directing my life. Maybe this was what I had thought about years earlier when I had a sense of something bigger coming in my future.

Actually, I had no idea just how big.

"Becca, I'm home. Where are you, sweetheart? How come you didn't answer the phone. I've been trying to call you for an hour."

Our new apartment was much bigger than the old motel suite, but it didn't take more than a minute to check each room and discover she wasn't there. Wherever she had gone, she hadn't left me a note or even a hint as to where she might be.

Now I began to worry. This was just not like her.

A phone call to Eddie might calm me down.

"Rebecca's not here, Eddie. I have no idea where she might be."

"Maybe she went shopping, buddy."

"Stores at the mall closed over an hour ago and she doesn't want to look at clothes until after the baby comes, so I don't think so."

"What about girl friends?"

"We haven't been here long enough to establish any friends outside of you and Christa."

"Did you try her doctor?"

"Yeah, I did. I even called the hospital. Not there either, thank God."

"You guys have a fight or something?"

"No, No, Nothing like that. This has never happened before. I'm worried, Eddie."

Ever the alert FBI agent, Eddie asked the jackpot question. "Do you see her purse around?"

"It's not here. I've already checked."

"Wait right there. Don't call anybody. I'll be right over. I'll grab a sandwich on the way. Can I bring you one?"

"Thanks. I'm not hungry."

"I know, but this may turn out to be a long night so I'm bringing you a burger. Want some French fries?"

"I guess so. Thanks."

It was just past eleven p.m. when Eddie arrived. He felt he had to explain that Christa had wanted to come too, but, because of the late hour, they had nobody to leave the children with, so she stayed with the kids.

"What do you reckon we should do, Eddie?"

"I'm beginning to think she may have been kidnapped."

"Oh, My God! She's pregnant and she's sick most of the time. What have you seen that makes you think she's been taken?"

"Well, she's not here. Didn't leave her 'scared to death' husband a note telling him where she's gone. She left a half-done dinner on the stove. You don't have to be Sherlock Holmes to believe she's been taken. I've been to a few training seminars on kidnappings that have this same MO. I've also known her for a while, even dated her while we were all in college, in case you forgot. Disappearing without notice just isn't in her DNA. Enough?"

"I am really scared. This can't be happening. Isn't there something we can do right now?"

"I don't mean to scare you or make fun of you. I think we should sit on this for a couple of hours and see if you might get a message of some sort."

Eddie was calm, and I really appreciated that....it made me feel a little less panicky. I was praying under my breath and that helped too. I had never prayed out of desperation before, but I was doing it now. And, even though I had told him I wasn't hungry, I woofed the hamburger and fries like I'd been on a voluntary fast.

Around midnight there was a knock on my front door. Eddie got it, and in walked two young FBI agents who Eddie introduced as Walter and Ted. Eddie explained they were here to provide security. I mentioned to Eddie that I wished they were going to be close in case of any trouble. Eddie let me know that they were now assigned to be here until Rebecca was found, and they could sleep in the spare bedroom we had in our condo. That would work.

Ted got busy rigging our phone with a recorder and tracer.

Eddie looked right at me. "Do you have a gun in the house?"

"Yeah, we both have one. I insisted we each get one after the break in we had. We had a little trouble getting our permits, but they finally came through. We both had lessons on gun safety when we were kids."

"Well, you need to go get yours and keep it on you when you're in the house."

I answered the call that came in at 1 a.m. It was not a voice or accent that I recognized.

"Jeffrey Allan, listen carefully. If you ever want to see your pretty wife again, you better do exactly what I am ordering you to do!"

"You have been sniffing around our operations, and we don't allow anyone to mess in our business. We know you work for the Feds and we know you have some influence. You are now going to use that influence to assist our organization. If you are not willing or able to meet our demands, you will never see your wife again. Do I make myself clear?"

"Very clear. What do you want me to do?"

"You will receive information in the next couple of days giving you our demands and instructions. You will have exactly seventy-two hours from then to follow through with what our requirements are."

"Let me repeat. If you fail to meet our demands, you will never see your wife again, not even to bury her."

"Do not call the cops or get your FBI buddy to help you or we'll just eliminate your wife right when we find out. I will get in touch with you and give you details of what we expect from you. There is no need for you to rig your phone. You will be contacted by the means I think will serve our purpose best, but I can assure you, it will not be by telephone."

"Now, I'm going to hang up. You won't hear from us again tonight."

The line went dead.

Eddie said he had some ideas, and left about 2 a.m. to go home. I didn't sleep a bit that night and dragged myself out of bed about 6 a.m. I didn't know what I could do but I had to do something. I had moved all my office stuff out of the spare bedroom to accommodate Walter and Ted, and I sat in our bedroom, trying to think of what my next move should be.

Around 9:00 a.m., the phone rang. It was Adolph Riddler of all people. My first reaction was that I had too much on my plate to be bothered by him right now, but the tone of his voice cautioned me to listen to what he had.

"I have some important information about your wife you will want to hear, but I don't dare tell you over the phone. You will just have to take my word for this right now. I've gotta tell you in person. Wire me $1,000 for me to buy a ticket and I'll be on the first plane from Amarillo this afternoon."

"Give me a number, and I'll call you right back, Adolph."

Walter and Ted came into the room for their morning coffee, and I told them about the call. They immediately called Eddie.

"Wire him the money, get his flight info, and tell him we'll pick him up in the baggage claim area."

Early that afternoon, I slipped out the back door into the garage, just as Eddie had instructed me. I drove to the FBI motorpool in Walter and Ted's car, and got in Eddie's government special issue SUV. It was huge, black and had the blacked-out windows.

"Eddie was the first to speak. "Do you know if Riddler likes coffee?"

"Oh, man. Does he!"

"Good. We'll pick him up a cup from Starbucks, on the way." Eddie had been schooled well in witness preparation.

We picked up Riddler and whisked him to our automobile, safely parked in the "No Parking Tow Zone" area. It was safely watched by a policeman buddy of Eddie's, a perk of the badge.

I tried to make "small talk" on the way to the car, but Riddler said nothing. I began to worry about his motive for coming. He pulled me aside.

"Look, I know you brought your guy there with you to Amarillo, but I'm uncomfortable with him listening to us because the guys we are dealing with are dangerous guys. They could get to him and under pressure he could identify me as talking with you. Then I'm dead. Do you hear me? I'm DEAD!"

If this wasn't such a serious matter, and if I wasn't under tremendous stress myself, I would have laughed. I needed to make him feel comfortable.

"Adolph, this is Eddie Cruise. He's an FBI agent as well as a personal friend of mine. He and I have been working this case together. I can assure you he can be added to your list of people you can trust."

"OK, good. I just needed to know who he was. I got a phone call yesterday morning from Ah Kum Jianguo, that same Oriental guy who threatened me in my office that I told you about."

Yeah. How could I forget the man who had either killed Joseph LaSalle, or had someone do it for him? He had tried to kill me too.

Once we arrived at Eddie's office and got Riddler and his coffee safely inside, he began to feel more comfortable. Eddie called in a stenographer to make a record of the meeting.

"Jianguo told me his people had your wife in their custody, and were working on a deal to get you guys to call off your investigations into the bankruptcy matters."

"I asked him 'Why tell me?' He told me he knew that you had come to Amarillo to look at my accounts, and he wanted to give me a 'heads up' to let me know that my worries about you finding anything was about to be taken care of."

"Now, Mr. Allan, I never told him or anyone else about what you and I had talked about when you visited last week, and Jianguo had no reason to think that I would betray them, unless he finds out I am here talking to you now."

Riddler now completely opened up and told us everything he knew about the conspiracy, and it was a ton! He took us on a trip down his memory lane, back to his college days at Berkeley. The four of them, he, Tony Santos, Sidney Witherspoon, and Leon Quirk were very close friends. They hung out together all the time. After his girl friend's death and his confrontation with her grandfather, who he now identified as Godfather Long Ziqlang, he intentionally drifted away and stayed that way until he was contacted by Ah Kum Jianguo at his Trustee office in Amarillo. There he learned of the close ties his three former fraternity brothers had with Long Ziqlang, an association which

Riddler had reluctantly joined. Several times the four met in San Francisco at the headquarters of Dragon Rules down on the waterfront. The group's objectives, and it was working Riddler claimed, were to infiltrate and control the federal bankruptcy system in the Bay area and to use the Trust accounts to subsidize other schemes like drugs, illegal immigration, and child smuggling and trafficking. They hoped to prove their power and influence among the immigrants by physically destroying an important Bay area landmark. They would do that soon, according to the now talkative but scared Riddler. He claimed he didn't know the identity of the landmark, but he was becoming an excellent conversationalist.

Eddie spoke up when Riddler finished. "Here, Adolph, sign this statement of fact about what you've told us."

"I'm not sure I want to sign it, Mr. Cruise. I might be signing my own death warrant if this would get out. You know what I mean?"

"Yeah, I do, but if you refuse to sign it, it'll go much tougher for you, particularly with the US Attorneys and the Judge." He signed it quickly.

Riddler, Eddie, and I got back in the SUV, and we headed for the waterfront. Riddler pointed out the warehouse building where Dragon Rules headquarters was, being careful to duck down in the back seat where his face couldn't be seen. He obviously didn't know that no one on the outside could see inside the car.

Afterwards, we took him back to the airport for his flight back to Amarillo. He needed to be there in case Ah Kum Jianguo came looking for him again. We gave him strict instructions not to tell anyone, not even his family, about meeting with us.

Eddie contacted FBI headquarters and brought them up to date on progress made in solving Rebecca's kidnapping. He recommended that Riddler be afforded Witness Protection status, and that he be labeled the "Government's Key Witness" as a result of his spilling his guts and signing the confession he had made.

Local authorities were now notified of the kidnapping, and later that night, Eddie, Walter, Ted, and I got together in our apartment to formulate a plan.

It had been twenty-four hours since the first call about Rebecca's abduction. Eddie took charge of planning the rescue operation. He stressed that no matter where she was being held, the rescue team couldn't just rush in like a Cavalry charge. The plan to rescue her had to be done with utmost care and precision, as there were two lives at stake--Rebecca and our unborn child. I pointed out that she had been having trouble sleeping and keeping food down for a while. No telling what her condition was now.

Several hours later, the comfort of being at home wasn't enough to calm my nerves. I had just laid down when there was a loud knock on the front door. I sent the FBI guys to the back room while I answered the door.

A young Chinese boy handed me an envelope and then quickly disappeared. Inside the envelope were my instructions to affect the release of Rebecca.

First, I had seventy-two hours to produce a $5,000,000.00 payment; second, the funds had to be delivered to the "Outback,

Inc." bank account in the Cayman Islands before the time limit expired; third, the US Government had to guarantee safe passage to North Korea for Dragon Rules leader, Long Ziqlang. Lastly, they demanded a letter signed by the Attorney General, dismissing all charges relating to bankruptcy investigations and criminal prosecution.

Tick, Tock. The seventy-two hour clock was now moving like a run-away train.

CHAPTER 16

Never Underestimate the Power of a Woman

W hen it comes to kidnapping, there's no other law enforcement agency in the world quite up to the Federal Bureau of Investigation. They've honed their skills over almost a century of unraveling and solving these crimes, ever since the infant son of Charles Lindberg was snatched from his home in New Jersey in 1932. Ever since that time, the FBI has had an entire division specializing in kidnapping and hostage situations. Their experience, methods, and track record of success are unrivaled, and their assistance is sought worldwide.

The careful planning by Eddie and his team, and the experience they had brought in dealing with kidnappings began to pay dividends.

Once the Chinese kid had left, Eddie got on his walkie-talkie to his agents parked at both ends of the block in the ubiquitous black Fords, to keep an eye on the Chinese kid on the bike. Those agents then notified a boyish-looking agent on a bicycle on the other side of the street from the Chinese courier.

He started keeping pace with the courier, blending in with other bicyclists who were also headed into the city either trying to beat the cost of transportation, or maybe just engaging in their favorite pastime.

The agent on the bicycle followed his target through Chinatown until the target disappeared through an overhead door into a dingy and unglamorous five-story warehouse building.

The FBI had been monitoring the movements in and out of the warehouse for two days. They observed that the warehouse was "guarded" by two adolescent male Chinese sentries who looked about as interested in the comings and goings as a couple of American teens would be. No other people were observable on site, and no lights were visible, save one. On the fifth floor at the front of the building was a room with six feet by six feet barred windows. Any observer could see that was the only room on the fifth floor with a light on. The FBI kidnap analysts opined that was where Rebecca was probably being held prisoner.

Back in my living room, the "Command Post" for the rescue mission, Eddie assembled the rescue team. In addition to me and Eddie, there were six other FBI guys, all experienced in hostage extraction. Only one in the room was inexperienced.... the husband of the victim. I was grateful to Eddie to be included, but my shirt was soaked thru and my knees were so rubbery that I had to sit down.

"Ok, guys. Listen up. Crunch time. Set your watches right now to six minutes after the hour." I couldn't grab the setting knob on my watch, but Walter noticed and did it for me.

"We have one advantage that they are completely unaware of. We know where they are, and how many of them there are and they do not know that we know. We're going to keep it that way. Now we have to figure out how best to rescue Rebecca without putting her life in any more danger than it already is."

It was understood that no one outside of the group in that room was to know of this mission. Rebecca's life hung in the balance. The fewer number of people who knew about what was happening meant fewer chances that word would leak out to the kidnappers.

Across from the warehouse was a public housing project. At Eddie's direction, I contacted the local authorities and was able to secure two apartments directly facing the warehouse. We were able to install Department of Defense Issue Night Vision cameras that enabled us to observe what the naked eye could not see. We could count the buttons on their shirts or the fillings in their teeth had we been so inclined. Added to the team was a Chinese-speaking lip reader, which enabled us to kind of figure out their conversations, most of which were pretty boring and irrelevant.

Eddie was setting the schedule and I admired the diligence and professionalism he brought to the task. Each agent had a specific place to be and job to do. That was Plan A. There was also a Plan B in the event the perps decided to move to another location. Nothing was being left to chance.

That evening our squadron of FBI agents, DEA agents and S.W.A.T. sharpshooters was stashed away in the apartment rooms with lights out but with several sets of infrared eyes on the warehouse building. Eddie was reluctant to involve me directly as I wasn't trained for this work. He didn't want me in harm's way, nor did he want me to somehow interrupt their mission. Nothing though could have prevented me from being a part of this group.

"Look, Jeffrey. You're involved emotionally in this and I respect that, but you are going to have to let us do our job the way we were trained."

"Yeah, I know. It's just that I'm so worried about her and this rescue operation could go badly. What can I do to stay informed and still not get in the way?"

"I'm going to have you monitor all of the movements of everyone once we get into the warehouse. You know the plan and you'll be in touch with me by Walkie-Talkie."

He sat me in front of a small TV-like screen, attached to a cable that was attached to what looked to me like an Enigma machine. Eddie explained the machine had already been programmed to track the movements of everyone in the warehouse building through heat sensors. It took me two or three tries, but with his instructions I learned how to follow everyone's movements once the raid began.

Late in the evening, the agents with the night vision goggles were able to make out several men meeting together in a room on the bottom floor of the warehouse. Pictures were taken and shown to Eddie and me for possible identification. Eddie was able to identify Sidney Witherspoon, Tony Santos, and Long Ziqlang. The "godfather" of Dragon Rules was finally making an appearance. The perps saw this as a big deal for them. They had no idea it was even a bigger deal for us!

The agents watched the upstairs room with the light, and they were able to count the men in the room with Rebecca, but could not identify any of them. There was also a very fit-looking Chinese woman in the room who apparently brought Rebecca food and water, and took her for brief breaks to the washroom. We did not overlook her as part of the gang.

"OK, guys. Listen up! It's 9:30 and we're on the clock. Let's review one last time everyone's mission."

"Zero hour is set for 2200, provided the perps are still meeting. If they finish before then, we'll hit them just when they start to break up."

"I've already divided you into two teams. Team 'BLUE', our DEA agents and US Marshalls will interrupt the perp's meeting, neutralize them, and take them into custody. I will lead Team 'RED', and our assignment is to reach the top floor via the inside stairs and the outside fire escape stairs before any of the perps have time to react. We will take any action necessary to rescue Rebecca, including putting down anyone who tries to interfere. Be sure to secure the woman who's with her. Lock her down."

The last twenty minutes seemed like an eternity.

At exactly 10:00 o'clock, the teams moved in.

Things got complicated right away. A lookout who had been hiding and was undetected by our group quickly alerted the perps who had been meeting, and they began to scatter. A member of the BLUE team saw someone in that group phoning out on his cell phone and several shots rang out. The perps were all scrambling up the inside stairway toward the top of the building.

In the meantime, I had been following everything on Eddie's machine, and it soon became too much for me to just watch.

I ran out of the apartment building and headed for the stairway below where Rebecca was. Eddie was in the stairway on his phone instructing the BLUE team leader to make sure none of the perps would escape. The rest of the RED team had already reached the top floor.

Shots rang out. I lunged past Eddie and headed for the top stairs with Eddie right behind me, shouting for me to wait for him. The top floor was the fifth floor, and ordinarily I would be out of breath by the time I climbed five sets of stairs. Not this time.

As we arrived, we heard shouting and shooting in the direction of the room where Rebecca was being held. We arrived at the room and saw two dead thugs on the floor. The RED team had already busted down the door and found a Chinese man racking the slide on his Glock 9mm.

Martial Arts training paid its first dividends to our family. From her seated position, Rebecca kicked him in the groin and then broke his knee. From the other side of the room, when he tried to fire again, he died in a hail of bullets from Eddie's gun. He had just earned another notch to his "Fast Eddie" nickname.

Rebecca leaped for joy as she first saw Eddie and then me. Someone threw a blanket over her shoulders, and we took turns, half carrying, half dragging her down the stairs. A waiting ambulance took us to the ER at St. Francis Hospital where Rebecca was examined, and fell asleep on the gurney from exhaustion. Her only injury was that vicious weapon at the end of her leg which had crushed her captor's knee.

The following morning, we were allowed to go to our apartment to rest for her upcoming FBI interview. She was badly shaken by her ordeal, but the only injury she had was her injured foot. We were both thankful it had ended as well as it had.

The next afternoon we were taken to FBI headquarters. There, Rebecca told the story of her abduction.

She had gone shopping and was returning to our car when she was approached by a woman and two men who forced her to their car.

"Just get into the car, and you won't be hurt."

They only told her that she was being held as a hostage and that in a couple of days she would be freed. "We're going to hold you in a big room and you'll be safe and comfortable. We'll bring you some good Chinese food from our restaurant and you'll have a bed to sleep in. You will be the responsibility of a woman about your age who has taught Taekwondo for many years. Don't mistake her gentle manner for softness. Do you understand?"

Once upstairs in the old warehouse, an older Chinese man who spoke perfect English assured her that she would not be harmed as long as "she did not cause trouble."

That was how Rebecca had wound up being kidnapped, but now it all seemed like ancient history. We decided the following day to put Rebecca on a plane to Atlanta. She could stay with her mother until I was completely finished with my assignment. She had been through enough traumas to last a lifetime and I was not going to leave her here in harm's way any longer.

Unfortunately, all of the principal people the BLUE Team had been assigned to capture in the warehouse raid had escaped. A waiting helicopter on the roof had been alerted by a phone call just as the raid began. As local agencies had not been notified and put on alert regarding the mission, there was no interception of the getaway helicopter. Agents tried during the raid to alert law enforcement of the escape, but were unsuccessful.

Eddie loved his 6 a.m. phone calls to me. "Hey, buddy. Rise and shine! We're only half way home. Lots of the bad guys got away and we still don't know what they were trying to do. Nobody's talking and I doubt they will. They all seem scared. I think it's because they all have families in China and they have been threatened. As you know, life means nothing to these people. I guess you can understand it when you realize they have over a billion people in the country."

When I got to Eddie's office, his outlook on the case had changed for the better. One of the older gang members, Huang Chen, had surrendered rather than be killed. He had become disillusioned with Long Ziqlang and the rest of the gang members. He was still fearful of Dragon Rules members, and was hesitant about telling what he knew about them. Still, he could become a very valuable asset to our team.

Chen was taken to FBI headquarters and grilled for several hours about the plans and activities of Dragon Rules. We wanted to find out about the roles of Witherspoon and Santos in their organization. At first, Chen wouldn't talk. So, the FBI decided to bring in someone from the counter-terrorist team to try and convince him.

In the meantime, gossip and speculation reigned supreme in the Bay Area regarding the raid on the Dragon Rules gang and their possible connection to the now public bankruptcy conspiracies. Television newscasters were interviewing anyone with a possible connection, and the newspapers printed several stories about what the editors described as a conspiracy against the United States Government.

A Grand Jury was convened by the Attorney General, and indictments followed. The head of the US Trustees office in San Francisco, Tony Santos, was publicly named, accused, and absently indicted, as was also one of the Bankruptcy judges, Sidney Witherspoon.

Speculation swirled throughout the community and a ravenous Press Corps. How could these well-credentialed, well-educated public servants have allowed themselves to be so thoroughly corrupted? Why would they risk their careers, families, and even their lives to such public disgrace? What was their agenda for their connection to the Chinese mafia organization, Dragon Rules?

What was the payoff??

CHAPTER 17

A Bridge Too Far

My "Tour of Duty" to the West Coast was finally winding down. I had already testified before the Federal Grand Jury regarding my involvement in the Witherspoon-Santos investigations and was in the process of wrapping up some loose ends before heading back to Georgia. The US Trustee's office was settling down too, as one of the Assistant US Trustees had been named Acting US Trustee, taking over Santos job. The office attitude was undergoing a transition; even receptionist Alice was mellowing somewhat. This relaxed atmosphere gave me an opportunity to become more conscious of my immediate environment.

There was more happening in the Bay Area to capture newspaper and television headlines than just the raid on Dragon Rules, and the disappearance of two high-ranking government officials. For several days, the media busied themselves with speculation about why rich and powerful lawyers would get involved in crime in Chinatown. A few days later, the daily drumbeat of muggings, murders and mayhem pushed our story off the Front Page and the ten o'clock news and back to normal. Or so I thought.

The Big News now was that US Vice President Jacob Moyers was coming to the Bay Area for a dedication ceremony of the San Francisco-Oakland Bay Bridge Eastern Span project.

Actual history can be a pesky and painful reminder. The Bay Bridge had partially collapsed when, just before the first pitch of Game 3 of the World Series at Candlestick Park on October 17, 1989, the baseball diamond began to crumble. This was the beginning of the Loma Prieta earthquake, which resulted in sixty-three deaths, most of whom had been trapped on the Bay Bridge and were either crushed by the fall of the roadbed above them or who were dumped into the shark-rich open waters of the Bay as the roadbed collapsed beneath them.

The bridge was subsequently repaired but it had only been a temporary solution. Several years later, the bridge was ruled unsafe by the California Department of Transportation. This resulted in the replacement of the entire Eastern Span.

It took eleven long years to complete the project, at a cost of $6.5 billion, a cost overrun of 2,500 percent from its original estimate of $250 million. Construction materials came from Sweden, China, and Japan, not exactly "locally sourced." The most sophisticated section came from China, and was a seldom-built, self-anchored suspension bridge, spanning the very top arch of the bridge. A large platform at the top of the span had been temporarily installed where the dedication ceremony was to take place.

The News Media trumpeted Vice President Moyers, a "local boy who made good," would be on hand to lead the celebration. He was the odds-on favorite to be the front-runner in next year's Presidential Sweepstakes. Since he was from Hillsborough, a suburb of San Francisco and a graduate of both Cal and Stanford Law School, all of the Bay Area political governments, Federal, State and Local, wanted the ceremony to come off without any problems to show the city and the Vice President in the most favorable light.

But that was all to be the next day, June 15th and it was still a day away. Today I just needed to have focus. I had been asked to participate in the interrogation of one of the perps we had captured in the warehouse, Huang Chen. I was not favorably disposed toward this sewer rat, which I saw was being at least partially responsible for imprisoning my sweet, innocent, and very pregnant wife.

Upon entering the FBI reception area, we were seated under the obligatory posed smiles of the President of the United States, the Attorney General of the United States, the Director of the FBI, and the Special Agent of Charge of the San Francisco FBI headquarters. All were frozen in intimidating perfection, as were all of us in dark suits and corporate ties. Where was the perp?

When we entered the interrogation room with its large mahogany table and straight-backed dark wood library chairs, my question was answered as a slight Oriental man in an orange jumpsuit rose to his feet, as if out of respect. I had a hard time even looking at him initially. I was determined to help get the truth out of him.

The FBI had provided us a pretty complete dossier, from his early years to the present time, as a near indentured servant of the notorious Long Ziqlang. The main points had been FBI verified that made them very reliable for us.

He declined coffee or tea or "designer water," but accepted a glass of still water from the tap and politely thanked the one who brought it, unlike the other four of us, who initially accepted our coffee or coke without so much as a show of gratitude. Then, after watching our prisoner's manners, we all chimed in, probably out of embarrassment.

Eddie began the interrogation. "So tell us, Huang Chen, how long have you known Long Ziqlang. When and where did you first meet?"

"We were friends as boys, in Taipei. We were neighbors and our parents were friends. His mother and father took me in when my parents went away with the Red Guard for vacation and re-education."

"How long were your parents gone?"

"I never saw them again, but the Comrade manager in our village told me they didn't want me and that me and my brothers were now on our own. That was common in our area. My father was a doctor and very independent."

Huang Chen spoke perfect English and had clearly been well-educated.

"The Long family took us in and cared for me. I was ill from TB....from the smokestacks, I think. We also burned coal in our houses for heat. The coal was a gift from Chairman Mao."

He had gone quickly from being a perp to a victim in my eyes. I remember telling myself that I was dealing with a crook, maybe a killer, maybe a drug dealer. "Don't go 'soft'", I silently warned myself.

"What then?"

"I went to university to become a doctor like my father, but the Commissar of Education told me the people had enough doctors, and they needed me to be a structural engineer to build great things that would bring honor to China."

My American cultural values inserted themselves: "Is that what you chose to do then?"

"Please understand: when there is no alternative, there is no choice. I went to Wuhan University and I graduated first in my class. They told me I was being assigned to Shanghai Zhenhua Heavy Industries Company where I would be working on big construction projects."

Eddie took over the questioning. "Did your wife go along with that?"

"How did you know about my wife? I didn't mention her."

For once, Eddie was at a loss for words, so he skipped the question and suggested, "It's time for a break, I think."

At long last, the FBI provided some food for us, some really good Corned Beef sandwiches from Manny's Deli down the street. As I woofed mine down American Style, I observed our Oriental friend sitting in front of a small bowl of rice. After a couple of bites and a few sips of water, he put down his chopsticks and stared out the window over the bay toward Alcatraz. I had originally thought him to be in his late forties or early fifties. He had a lot more miles on him than that. Heartache takes a toll, in any culture, at any time. It doesn't need permission to extract life from us.

When we resumed, Huang Chen was composed, but damp-eyed.

"Then surely you know from your file that my wife is dead from a house fire. My son and twin daughters were sent by The Party to a special school. You do know that, at your FBI, do you not?"

"I prefer to be the one asking questions, but yes, we do know that, but we thought your wife was killed in a fire in a Christian Church. She was the leader of the home church there, right?"

"I'm not allowed to talk about that. Officially, it was a house fire from a fireplace that overflowed into the room."

"How old would your children be today?"

"My son would be thirty and my daughters twenty-eight."

"And how long has it been since you heard from them?"

"Twenty-four years, eight months, and eleven days."

"What then?"

"Then I went to live with the Long family and I worked on building big bridges all over the country. I became a Supervisor of Engineers at Shanghai Zhenhua Heavy Industries. The Long family became an 'Enemy of the People' and I was terminated from my job for my association with them. I was sent to the countryside to work on the railroads, laying track for high-speed trains. I tried to find my children, but I could not. I was able to contact Long Ziqlang who was in America and he wanted me to come work for him. He had a secret company, he said, named 'Dragon Rules'. The Dragon is a much-respected symbol in China, standing for Power and Honor. He told me he could get me a visa. He needed someone he could trust to help with a special engineering project he was planning. Two weeks later, I was here."

"Let's go back to your time with Shanghai Zhenhua. What did you do there?"

"We copied from X-ray photographs of the structure of major bridges around the world. The photographs were taken by Chinese businessmen who toured cities where there were big new bridges. They brought the photos back to China and my specialty was turning them into engineering drawings that we could use in our projects. It took a long time to get them right, but not as long as if we had to create the design specs ourselves."

"Did it ever cross your mind you might be doing something illegal?"

"By whose laws? It wasn't illegal in China. In fact, copying details is a highly paid profession in China. We copy everything. The Party even has special awards and compensation for people who can do it perfectly. We even have a word for it in Mandarin, 'T'Sungxhi', and it's usually reserved for those who work for Pottery Companies who make copies of ancient porcelains and are sold to the tourists. I had about 100 such copiers working for me and I was well rewarded."

"Did you make bridge parts?"

"Yes, we did and sold them all over the world to architects and engineers. They put their own stamps on them as their own and no one objected."

"Did you know whom the bridges were being copied for?"

"I never kept any record of customers the bridge parts were made for because that wasn't my job. I do know we made a special bridge span for one of your bridges here in San Francisco."

"Did you ever try to sabotage anything to do with any bridges you were working on?"

"No. That would be immoral. I never tried to sabotage anything. That could harm people."

As the day ended and they led Huang Chen back to his cell, I had a strong feeling inside that was hard to describe.... that something wasn't right,.....something that didn't come out in the interrogation. Something he wasn't telling us. A missing piece that we didn't get from Huang Chen. I felt drawn to work to try and discover what that "still small voice" inside of me was trying to say......a voice that was sounding louder by the minute.

Maybe I was losing my mind.

I got home and wasn't hungry, and besides, that Corned Beef Sandwich was still talking to me. Maybe that was the 'still small voice' I heard.

I lay in bed trying to understand that voice that wouldn't shut up. I thought back to other times in my life when I felt this Presence.

The first time was when I was almost killed by a big boulder coming through my windshield when I was on my way to my first embezzlement assignment in Maine. Then, later in McAllen, Texas, I barely escaped death again. How impossible did it now seem that after being thrown out of a moving car traveling almost 100 miles an hour that I would have survived by landed in a drainage ditch and going undetected by the men who were trying their best to make sure I was dead? Something definitely protected me, and that same "still small voice" led me to safety, away from those trying to kill me.

It showed up again to lead us to the Dragon Rules hideout and the rescue of my Rebecca. What about how I got to be in on the rescue of Rebecca, let alone my being there and getting to console her after the rescue. Again, that Powerful Force, that voice inside of me was urging me to go further to find the answer.

Lying down and getting quiet wasn't easy, especially with this out-of-control voice interrupting my every thought. My mind was racing and my analytical Accountant's brain was traveling full speed ahead. I was finally able to shift my thoughts back to what was happening now. I even asked God to help me. I was finally able to drift to sleep.

I awoke and looked at my watch. It was 4:30. Still a couple of hours to sleep if Eddie didn't call me at 6. My mind, though, turned on again.

I went over in my mind everything that had occurred since I was sent out here from Washington. The Leon Quirk bankruptcy fraud, the Judith Quarles matter, the murder of Leon Quirk, the abduction of Rebecca, the murder of Dexter Freeman.

WAIT!! I suddenly had a new thought. That might be it.

I recalled the sheet of paper in an envelope located in the bank safe deposit box. I had made a copy of it in my notebook I was keeping on the case for each day. Looking frantically, I found my notes for that day. I read the cryptic notation: "BB-veep-6/15". At first, I didn't have the foggiest notion. It was now approaching daylight on June 15th. Maybe it referred to today? Weird, huh.

I recalled a television sitcom that Rebecca and I had watched a few times called "Veep," about a fictional Vice President of the United States. Maybe that's what "veep" stands for. Then I remembered. The Vice President was coming to San Francisco today, June 15th.

Now, for the first part; "BB." It could stand for Big Boy, couldn't it? After all, the Vice President was one of the biggest personalities around. Yeah, that might be it. What else? BB. A BB gun? Not likely.

Suddenly it struck me like a bolt out of the blue.

Bay Bridge? That's it! BINGO.

Not a second to waste. The Vice President was going to dedicate the Bay Bridge today in just a few hours.

The California Department of Transportation had the responsibility for the construction project. They also had the Bay Bridge construction specifications, but it was only 5 a.m., and I was only a short drive away. I picked up a morning paper which told me the dedication was set for 2:30. For security reasons the actual dedication could be as much as a half hour either side of 2:30.

About 6 a.m., a police car pulled up beside me. There was a uniform on either side of me.

"What are ya doing out here this early, Pal? Let's see some ID, and put your hands on the steering wheel where I can see them."

"I'm waiting for the DOT to open. I've been involved in the 'Dragon Rules' investigation with the Department of Justice, and I need to check something out."

"I'm not sure that makes any sense. I think you had better lock up your car and get in the car with us. We'll take you down to our Precinct and see if we can sort this out."

I did as I was told. We weren't far from the station.

In their interrogation room, I showed them my ID from the US Trustee's office. Federal ID cards are a big deal out away from Washington DC, and I suspected officers Kelly and Koslowski had never seen one. Nor had their boss, Sgt. Wilheim, nor had the Precinct Night Supervisor, Cpt. Mickelberry. They all wanted to know what bankruptcy had to do with Cal D.O.T.

I was running out of patience and time, so I gave them the Beeper and Emergency Home Phone of Special Agent Eddie Cruise and suggested they should "call him, Right Here, Right Now. I can't tell you any more." Eddie had always told me this tactic would unplug the sewer of local nonsense and further, "do not hesitate to use it if you need to." It also got me a fast cup of coffee and the offer of a donut.

Eddie arrived about thirty minutes later with antenna out. He didn't have a clue what I was doing waiting for the California Department of Transportation to open up, but he pretended to my captors that it was all part of the ongoing investigations I was involved in. Fast Eddie was fast on his feet too.

They released me but I'm not sure they understood Eddie's story. On the other hand, he was FBI, and so they didn't argue.

Once safely out of earshot, Eddie started with the questions.

"Jeff, what in Blue Blazes was that all about? What were you doing at Cal DOT?"

I told Eddie everything including reminding him what the message read and the possible implications. That got his attention real fast.

"You should have called me and told me this. The FBI is set up to react quickly to national emergency situations, and you are not. You need to let us do our job."

"Eddie, I was just listening to the 'still small voice' inside me that told me that something wasn't right."

"OK, great. Just don't put that in your report, OK? The Bureau might just ship me off to a nice quiet office like Paducah."

We went to the San Francisco office of the California Department of Transportation, and Eddie got a copy of the bridge specs. There in black and white was the exact location where the Vice President would be standing during the dedication ceremonies, alongside the name of the bridge manufacturer, Shanghai Zhenhua Heavy Industries Company of China. BINGO!

The plot was thickening. This bridge had indeed traveled too far.

CHAPTER 18

Final Jeopardy: Class Reunion In Hell

"You knuckleheads haven't stopped anything yet," the Attorney General roared. "The three main conspirators on the loose, you tell me of a possible assassination plot against the Vice President, and a 6.5 billion dollar bridge that's about to go down. You know, the taxpayers of this country won't want to build it again....again. So, what have you got? I can call off the whole event right now and route all traffic away from the bridge, but then what? How credible do you think your hunch is, Jeff? And right now that's all it is...a hunch. This is what I would call a NNN Triple Header, a National News Nightmare, and it's happening on the front end of an election season. The press is about ready to eat our lunch. You two had better figure this thing out or I'm gonna eat yours first. Keep a line open. I want every detail." Click.

Eddie added factually. "That's why he makes the big bucks. Let's get busy."

We started laying out ideas, trying to come up with how the plot might work and how to stop it. We needed some fresh thinking, some new idea, maybe a word from the "still small voice" that had invaded my thought patterns recently.

Rebecca was on the phone…just what I needed at that moment.

"I can't talk now, Honey. We've got a crisis here. We think there might be a plot to blow up the Bay Bridge and the Vice President this afternoon, and we haven't figured out yet how they're going to do it, with what…from where…"

"Have you asked that little Chinese man you told me about last night? Didn't you tell me he once worked for the company that built the bridge span?"

The phone dropped out of my hand without another syllable as I headed for Huang Chen's cell, telling myself: "Boy, am I glad I sympathized with his story yesterday. I think my instincts were right about him. He has been a victim of their insidious culture for a long time. He should be in the mood to help us."

I rounded the corner to the cell block and saw there was someone else in the cell with Huang Chen: Attorney Peter Seabolt.

"My client and I need privacy now, Mr. Allan. You should leave until we are through."

"Just a minute now. Mr. Huang has been cooperating with us the entire time he has been here, and we know he hasn't asked to make any outside calls, so why are you here?"

"Huang Chen is an important principal in the company he works for, and the shareholders have hired me to represent him."

By now, Eddie had joined us. "Huang Chen, do you want to be represented by a lawyer?"

"No, Sir. I do not. I was telling Mr. Seabolt before Mr. Allan showed up that I was through with their organization, but Mr. Seabolt insisted that he represent me. I don't want that. I don't want to see innocent people hurt. I want him to leave." Turning to Seabolt, Chen continued. "Please leave me alone."

"Ok, little man, you will learn the hard way. They're going to lie to you to make you talk, and then they're going to send you off to prison somewhere and you'll never see the light of day again. But hey. It's your funeral." With that, Peter Seabolt rose from his seat, walked to the cellblock door and left, slamming the door behind him.

Eddie led Huang Chen back to the same conference table we were at the day before. This time, the Chinaman had a cup of hot tea waiting for him.

At Eddie's insistence, I began the questioning. "Huang Chen, can you help us figure this thing out? It may be a matter of life or death."

"Good morning to you, too, Jeffrey. I slept well until that lawyer your FBI let in here came and bothered me, but thanks for asking."

"So sorry for my bad manners, but there's a problem here that you might have the answer to. There will be thousands of innocent men, women, and children on the Bay Bridge this afternoon so I need to ask you a few questions."

"Yesterday you told us that Shanghai Zhenhua built a bridge span for a bridge in the San Francisco area. We know that bridge was the Bay Bridge. Did you supervise the building of that span?"

"Yes."

"Now for a theoretical question. If you wanted to blow up the bridge, how would you do it? Could you do it?"

"Yes. With every bridge there is a weakest point. Now the span on the Bay Bridge was constructed to be strong enough to withstand a nine magnitude earthquake, but anything built by man can be destroyed. You just have to know how to do it."

"And so how would you bring down the Bay Bridge?"

"You have to locate the weakest point, and I know where that is. Not that it is weak or flawed in the traditional sense. Think of it this way. Let's say there are 1000 key structural points the bridge. They are all strong. They have been tested and all are safe. But, among them there is one point that is the weakest. We know that if that point were to be put under maximum stress, say an earthquake of 9.1, which point is the one that is most likely to fail. It is important in structural design as well as emergency procedures to know this."

"Will you tell me where the weak point is on the Bay Bridge? Can you lead us to it? Can you help us?"

"Yes, I know the spot. Yes, I can lead you to it. Yes, I can help you. But first, I need some help from you." Huang Chen just went from Victim to Victor. He turned and faced Eddie. "Mr. FBI man, you threatened me yesterday with twenty years in prison if I didn't cooperate, but you never said what would happen if I did cooperate."

"What do you want? We're sort of a hurry here."

"You Americans are always in a hurry for what you want."

"Mr. Allan and I talked about you last night. I'm going to talk to the federal prosecutor, the US Attorney, and recommend that they seek minimal prison time if you will cooperate with us to get these guys."

"Even more important to me is finding my children and getting them to safety. Is there any way you can help me with that?"

"Well, as you can imagine, that will be very difficult given that your children disappeared years ago and China is so mysterious and big. But we will try and find them."

"Will you put that in writing?"

"I can't. It wouldn't mean anything if I did. I will recommend to the Attorney General that we engage some assets to try and locate them."

Less than thirty minutes later, the Attorney General had the Director of the Central Intelligence Agency on the phone to say they would give it a 100 percent effort. That was good enough for Huang Chen.

"Thank you for not threatening me. I will help you."

I think I learned something new about working with people, about using Honey instead of Anchovies, or something like that. Rebecca was fond of saying "do unto others." Is that what it meant?

More than that, could we trust Chen?

It was now 1:30 and the dedication was scheduled for an hour from now. We had to trust Chen. We had no other choice.

Once the architectural plans were on the table, Chen pointed out the "Guest Platform," with the well-concealed access panel.

"When I was working at Shanghai Zhenhua, my most important project was the Bay Bridge span. We had never had a project that was so difficult, so big, and so expensive. We won the bid over some big international construction companies like Bechtel, Skanska, Saudi Heavy Metal and we were going to prove we belonged in that group. My boss was anxious to prove China's superiority over other nations and was pressuring me to meet deadlines set forth in the contract. We worked long and hard to do that and to be thought of as good members of the Chinese Communist Party. You Americans call them the CCP. Well, I did that, and one day after five years, I was on a train to Wuhan, out of a job, and in disgrace for 'disloyalty to the Chairman and the Chinese people.' I went from 'Exalted Structural Engineer' to 'Apprentice Street Sweeper' overnight. I was angry and I swore I would get even one day."

"Long Ziqlang was still my friend and I contacted him to see if he could help me find my kids and he responded by getting me a US visa, a job with his company, and his promise to help me find my children. I did whatever he asked, including some smuggling of people and drugs. I realize now those things were not noble. I told him my thoughts. He told me, 'If you ever wanted to see your kids again you will do what I ask you to do, and keep your mouth shut.' I did that."

"I had told him about how I had gotten fired from the best job I ever had, designing the Bay Bridge, and that it had a secret compartment. Since he knew that things like this were part of the

Chinese culture for thousands of years, he asked me if I could still find it if I needed to. I thought that might be my way to get back at Shanghai Zhenhua and ruin their business and reputation in the world community."

"When I showed Long Ziqlang the compartment on the drawings, he knew instantly that it was located at that 'weak spot' of the bridge. I told him how to access it and one night he and a group of his men climbed the bridge from a small boat, loaded the compartment with a new version of C4 explosives, enough to bring down the entire span and cause massive fatalities. He said he could detonate it from mid-air in a helicopter within a couple of miles of the bridge. He wanted to wait for the right event to set it off."

"Later, I overheard Long Ziqlang discussing a plan to detonate the explosives from a helicopter hovering above the Golden State Bridge, about five miles away, as Vice President Moyers was delivering the dedication speech."

Well, there it was. We had almost a half hour to stop the Vice President from reaching the dedication platform.

Then Murphy's Law swung into high gear.

The lights went out in the building.

The air conditioning system shut down.

The office phones all went dead.

Cell phones didn't work.

"Jeffrey! Let's get out of here now. I'll meet you in the lobby."

Eddie and I had to scramble down ten flights of stairs to the bottom. Outside, I was able to call 911 who switched me to a dispatcher. The dispatcher put me on hold. It seems she was the only one left in the office as everyone else was at the dedication ceremony, and she was being swamped with emergency calls about the power outage. Then she apparently forgot we were on hold. I had to hang up and hit the re-call button.

"Lady, please don't put me on hold again," I all but shouted. "We have a 'life or death' situation here and I have to talk to the Secret Service right now!"

Completely misunderstanding me, she immediately notified police authorities about a man threatening the Vice President, and gave the authorities the source address of the call.

Eddie and I were quickly surrounded by about fifteen unfriendly faces on bodies with guns drawn! "We're FBI on the Vice President's security detail and we need an escort to get to the Bay Bridge. NOW!"

One of the teams of officers happened to be the two guys who had stopped me this morning in front of the Department of Transportation building. As they had already verified our identity, they let us climb into the back seat of their cruiser and we headed for the bridge, sirens and lights announcing our presence and urgency.

2:20 p.m. We saw the motorcade turning on to the bridge ahead of us. Eddie was on the phone now with the head of the Secret Service detail. The only way they could get the car with the Vice President to turn around was to get to the span section where the bomb was. Sharpshooter Agents had been alerted to scan the skies for the helicopter, but it had not yet been spotted.

The Black SUV carrying the Vice President arrived at the turn around just as the helicopter was spotted just above the horizon, just past the Golden State Bridge. Unknown to the passengers in the helicopter, the SS Des Moines had been alerted to the danger. It was stationed just to the West of the Golden State Bridge and had an electronic bead on the outlaw helicopter. When it got within range, the Des Moines locked on it and took it out. At impact, it scattered body parts and metal into the Bay below. Unfortunately, the Coast Guard did not have enough time to clear the area of pleasure boat traffic, and two boats with vacationing sightseers were also damaged and sunk. Civilian casualties always occur during times of war, and this was war.

Eight Navy SEALS from SEAL Team 5, stationed on the Des Moines, retrieved the lifeless bodies of Sidney Witherspoon, Tony Santos, and the notorious Long Ziqlang along with three members of their gang from the shark bait waters of the bay. They were also able to rescue about half the passengers from the damaged pleasure boats.

As usual, an FBI full investigation followed which is routine at the end of any mission. Eddie ran the investigation and introduced me as an "invaluable member of the team." I was grateful for that, but otherwise was a fly on the wall, and a very relieved one at that.

During the investigation, facts emerged that showed that Witherspoon, Santos, and Leon Quirk had been radicalized by the organization, Dragon Rules, probably while still in college. The FBI found that Dragon Rules had become a "Terrorist Organization" within the terms of the Federal Criminal Statute, financed in part by the North Korean Government, and in part by the Bay Area bankruptcy corruption practices. The objective of their organization was to "wreck havoc on whatever arm of government they could infiltrate." That infiltration turned out to be in the Federal Bankruptcy Court and System operating in the Bay Area. It began when Witherspoon, Santos, and Quirk became friends with Long Ziqlang. Their association in this organization intensified once Witherspoon, Santos, and Leon Quirk were employed by the bankruptcy system. Quirk got greedy and started stealing for his own needs, and that's when the whole deck of cards began to crumble. The deposits of money coming from the Swiss banks had their origin in North Korea and had been "washed" by several countries before the funds ever got to the Swiss banks, as Switzerland has a strong policy of not touching money from a terrorist state. The funds going to the Cayman Island banks and then to the corporate shell "Outfront" were funds used by Dragon Rules to purchase the most expensive helicopter available to civilians, and to provide fire power and living expenses to the Dragon Rules participants.

At the conclusion of the final investigative meeting, Eddie was in the process of introducing me to explain the Bankruptcy System implications, and as I was rising, the door swung open and in came two Secret Service officers followed by Vice President Moyers.

"Gentlemen and Ladies of this Joint Task Force, I apologize for breaking into your meeting. I was on my way to the airport when I realized I had forgotten to thank all of you, especially Jeffrey Allan and Eddie Cruise, for their extraordinary work and exemplary courage in breaking up this plot. These were some really bad actors that had been undetected and undeterred for years on several continents and in many jurisdictions in our country. I don't even know how you were able to unravel it all, but you did. I'm recommending both of you for the Department of Justice Service Medal, our highest honor, and to you, Jeffrey Allan, the Citizen Certificate of Valor, and to you, Eddie Cruise, The Peace Officer Certificate of Valor. Besides breaking up this bunch of crooks, you saved my life and I'm most grateful."

When I called Rebecca at the end of that session, I told her how grateful I was to be with a "Support Agency" of the government as opposed to an "Enforcement Agency" like the FBI. She seconded my motion.

"You wouldn't believe how that 'Still Small Voice' came to my rescue time and time again, all throughout this ordeal." She answered, "Why wouldn't I believe it? That same voice speaks to me all the time, darling."

Then it was time to say "goodbye," and head back home to Helen, Georgia to my beautiful and now very pregnant wife, Rebecca. Eddie told me he was allowed to take with me a copy of the confidential final report, which she and I would read together, and I would fill in the gaps as we went along.

I feel fortunate to have lived through this, and now I am headed home where I intend to stay for as long as I can. I don't know if I will ever go back to San Francisco, and Eddie told me as I was leaving, "I don't think we ever want to see you back here because you bring too much trouble!" I hoped he was kidding.

CHAPTER 19

Unexpected Consequences

I t's the "World's Busiest Airport," Hartsfield-Jackson International Airport, named for two former mayors of the city, William Hartsfield and Maynard Jackson. The rush of people with Starbucks in one hand and suitcase in the other, having to move at speeds faster than humans are comfortable, the relentless harsh sounds of flight announcements and excessive PSA's, robotic underground trains, all with smells of the worldwide kitchen. It amounts to an assault on the senses.

As a fairly regular traveler, I thought I was ready for all that.

What I wasn't prepared for was a gaggle of honking journalists waiting at the gate, for their town's newest and most unlikely hero, a reserved, average-looking accountant more interested in seeing his wife than meeting with them. There were about twenty of them ready to feast on just one of me.

"Mr. Allan, what's it like to break up a terrorist cell?"

"How many of the Chinese gang did you kill personally?"

"Is it true that your wife got sent back home because she was friends with some of the terrorists?"

"Are you seeing a marriage counselor?"

"Are there gangs here in Atlanta?"

"Did Vice President Moyers promise you a position in his administration if he wins the election next year?"

On and on it went for almost an hour. That's when two guys showed up and cleared me out of there through a side door, and into a car that looked like the one government officials drove in San Francisco….a big, black Ford SUV with blackened windows and US plates.

I was dizzy with stimulation. My rescuers handed me a note.

"You're a Celebrity…for the moment. I thought you would appreciate these guys more than flowers. Your bags are in the trunk, Pal. Becca and I changed your phone number to 404-555-5955. Call me tomorrow. EC."

And I guess I was a celebrity of sorts, maybe just a curiosity, something to talk about and fill newspaper columns and talk shows for a few days. Wasn't sure I liked it much. Definitely not comfortable with it.

The only phone call once we got out of the airport was to Becca.

"Whew. I'm on the ground, I think. This is crazy. How are you feeling?"

"Dr. Franklin's got me on bed rest for a week. Just a precaution. Nothing wrong, just playing it safe. My mom is here, but she'll be going home as soon as you get here. She's been a big help."

"Did the Doctor say how the baby is doing?"

"Yeah, they're fine."

"What did you say? Did you say 'they?'"

"I'll tell you all about it when you get here."

And that is how the mystery of new life began in Helen, Georgia.

The following day, however, had no understanding or respect for that new life. Though we slept until noon, the rest of the world demanded immediate attention.

"As your boss, I did think you would tell me that you were home and that you had a new phone number. I had to call Cruise to get it. When were you going to fill me in? Anything I should know?"

"Only that we're expecting twins, sir."

"Wow. That's great. Congratulations. I suppose that will bump up our insurance premiums quite a bit." Always the caring supervisor.

"You probably saw your picture and the story of your arrival on the front page of the AJC this morning."

"No, sir, I was frankly more concerned with my pregnant wife."

"Well, it mentioned you were up for some big award that was going to be given to you at the White House."

"First I've heard of it."

"You might want to mention to your friends in the Press that you work for the EOUST and not the FBI. They got all the credit, but I'm sure the AG knows."

"I'm sure he does. Say 'hello' to him from me if you get a chance."

"Will do. And he had some ideas for you to work on, new projects and cases. I want you to take the rest of this week off, but I would like for you to get your butt up here Monday morning to discuss my ideas. Say 10 o'clock? We can have lunch afterwards on the UST checkbook. Just the two of us."

"That's fine, sir."

This was something new, more than just new cases and projects. I wondered what was up? Becca would have a good idea or two and I was anxious to hear them.

"Callaway's probably got two things on his mind. He doesn't want to lose you to the FBI. He knows switching agencies would bump you up a couple of pay grades, so I think he will offer you some more money to do a different job, and I'll bet he's going to question you about your 'instinct' that leads you to locating corruption cases."

"I don't know where that comes from either. I think I just have to 'think like a crook'".

"Don't go getting worldly on me, Cordell. You know exactly what I mean. You haven't talked with anyone about 'talking to God', or 'hearing that still small voice' have you?"

"Only to Eddie."

"That's ok. He's safe. Krista and I have been talking about this for a while now. You just don't want to mention something that someone could misinterpret and make a note of it in your Personnel file."

"Oh, really? Where have I been?"

"I've brought it up several times, but you were busy with work stuff or too tired to take it all in. Or else, you just thought I was trying to talk to you about church or religion or something and changed the subject. I just didn't want to push it because I figured God would get your attention sooner or later on some case. And it looks like He did. I just don't think you ought to be talking about it around the office."

"You're probably right."

"So just be careful with Callahan. Listen and be grateful, but don't commit to anything. We'll talk about it when you get home from Washington."

Turns out Becca was right....again. Callahan offered me a supervisory position and a "Bump" in salary of 24 percent, which was maximum allowable raise. And he promised there would be more coming "next year" or "soon" when the regs permitted it. Accepting his offer would require us to leave Helen and move to Washington DC and would involve a considerable amount of travel, mostly overnight.

"Thank you, sir. I appreciate your confidence in me. As you know, Becca and I will become parents soon, and we need to evaluate the impact on our family."

Rebecca and I put a pencil to the offer and we determined by the time we absorbed the higher cost of living in the DC area we wouldn't be making as much as I was making now. It would also mean leaving our home which we truly loved. All of this plus Rebecca's decision to resign from her law firm in order to become a "stay-at-home" mom made our decision easy.

Then the Justice Department came-a-courting. They decided they needed a program for them to train all their attorneys across all departments on how to spot financial crimes before they ripened into big cases, and they asked me to write it for them. This was a project that would take about two years to complete. I asked if I could do this as an independent contractor, and they agreed, but they had to put it out to the public for bids. My bid was accepted, and I resigned my position with the EOUST and opened an office in Atlanta, hanging out my shingle as a forensic accountant.

Then another blessing showed up in the form of Eddie Cruise, who'd been transferred to Atlanta. We hadn't lost touch at all and talked at least once a week about what we were doing in life. He and Krista had three kids now and he needed a less stressful professional life more than chasing bad actors who didn't mind hurting those who got in the way of their schemes.

We partnered up and opened an office in North Atlanta, called "Cruise and Allan", specializing in helping financial institutions and charities keep their money safe for the use of their own clients.

Of all the people I had contact with in San Francisco, the only one I have kept up with is Huang Chen. The State Department and the International Committee of the Red Cross were able to finally locate one of his daughters. She was issued a visa and came to the United States, arriving just as her father was being released from a minimum security prison. She was able to find work as a seamstress and works from her home where she cares for Huang Chen who is no longer able to care for himself. They are still searching for his other children.

In the evenings from our log home in Helen, after we have tucked away to sleep our precious three-year-old boy and girl, Rebecca and I retire to our swing on our front porch where we have our quiet time....with ourselves, and with our Maker.

Often times I find myself re-living my past experiences that took me to Maine, New Jersey, Salt Lake City, Mississippi, Tennessee, Texas, and San Francisco. I think about the close encounters with death I had experienced; first, on my way to the airport in Georgia when a boulder came crashing through my windshield, then, being thrown from a car going 100 MPH on a back road in Texas, and finally, having to endure the anguish of a husband whose wife had been kidnapped and threatened with death.

Re-living these experiences makes me realize just how truly blessed Rebecca and I are. At first, I didn't understand it at all. There was nothing in my early life that suggested a Supernatural Power greater than me that controlled the universe. Growing up, my knowledge of God was limited to church Sunday School which my uncle and aunt who lived across the road took me to until I got to the age where I revolted against it. My folks were good people, but they were so tied up in their own problems the word "God" was not a part of their vocabulary, so I grew up with a very limited spiritual background and was just kind of left to try and figure things out my myself. Rebecca, prior to her parent's divorce, was brought up in a Christian environment. Before we got married, I had attended a church in Helen when I wasn't traveling all around the continent, mostly because that's what the good and respectable people in Helen did, and I wanted to fit in. After we got married, we began to attend regularly. This was driven, half by my curiosity, and the other half by my wanting to just be with her. One day I found myself asking the pastor if I could meet with him.

I explained to him everything I had gone through during my employment with EOUST, including the episodes with danger that culminated with the demise of Dragon Rules. The pastor listened intently, and when I finished, he asked me what I had learned from those experiences. I replied that I learned there was a Higher Power that had helped me through those many trials.

He told me he was going to write a prescription for me, one that should last me a lifetime. This is what he handed me:

Jeremiah 29:11. "For I know the plans I have for you," declares the Lord, "plans to prosper you and not to harm you, plans to give you hope and a future."

We ended our visit with him telling me I was always welcome to see him again. I told him he could count on it.

This, I have embedded in my memory bank. I take my notepad out often and refresh my mind with His promise.

My life priorities have completely changed now that I am surrounded by my family. They are the most important things in my life. I will always remember my experiences in San Francisco. My heart, though, is not there. It is with my family in Helen, Georgia.